P9-DEP-447

MiLLA TAKES CHARGE

By ERIN SODERBERG
Illustrated by ANOOSHA SYED

Random House  New York

rhcbooks.com

Library of Congress Cataloging-in-Publication Data
Names: Soderberg, Erin, author.
Title: Milla takes charge / by Erin Soderberg.
pages cm — (Daring Dreamers Club ; 1)
Description: "Like Belle, Milla loves nothing more than imagining bold adventures in the great wide somewhere. It's up to the rest of the Daring Dreamers Club—Piper, Zahra, Mariana, and Ruby—to help Milla prove she is ready for a real grand adventure!" —Provided by publisher.
Identifiers: LCCN: 2018001619 — ISBN 978-0-7364-3924-4 (hardcover) — ISBN 978-0-7364-3881-0 (lib. bdg.) — ISBN 978-0-7364-3882-7 (ebook)
Subjects: Adventure and adventurers—Fiction. | Camps—Fiction. | Princesses—Fiction. | Clubs—Fiction. | Friendship—Fiction. | BISAC: JUVENILE FICTION / Media Tie-In.
Classification: LCC PZ7.S685257 Mil 2018 | DDC [Fic]—dc23

Printed in the United States of America
10 9 8 7 6 5 4 3 2 1

*For Mom and Dad, with love.
Thanks for always encouraging me
to dream big.
—E.S.*

FIVE REAL GIRLS DARING TO DREAM
LIKE THE *Princesses* THEY *love*!

Piper

Tiana

Mariana

Ariel

Milla

Belle

Ruby

Mulan

Zahra

Cinderella

1
PRiNCE PiGGY

"Once upon a time, in a land far, far away, there lived a handsome prince. . . ." Milla Bannister-Cook plunked down on the ground and watched as her pet pig, Chocolate Chip, trotted through the backyard. She chewed the cap of her pen and waited, hoping Chip would do something interesting so she could come up with the next line of her story. Luckily, it never took very long for Chip to spring into action.

Milla had set up the yard so it looked like a miniature fairy-tale world. Her old dollhouse was the castle, potted plants served as trees, and a family of dolls had been given the roles of humble servants. She had even placed a plastic crown on her pig's head, hoping a costume would help Chip get into character.

But that morning, Milla's prince didn't feel like playing his part. It seemed the only thing the pig wanted to do was *destroy* his land. As Milla watched, Chocolate Chip—who'd gotten his name because Milla thought his brown-and-white-spotted coloring looked like a chocolate chip cookie—began trampling shrubs and toppling flowerpots. Then he overturned the castle and pushed his royal subjects into his empty food dish.

Milla read aloud as she scribbled, "The prince in *this* fairy tale was a little different from most storybook heroes. He wasn't always graceful, he wasn't very clean, and he ate like a pig." Chip turned and grunted at Milla. She giggled, adding, "But he was sweet, strong, and extremely lovable. You just had to get to know him first. Prince

Chip's friends knew this great beast was very cuddly and always treated his family and friends like royalty. He also loved to share his beloved toys and blankets on cold nights . . . most of the time."

Chip darted across the yard when he noticed Milla pulling a banana from behind her back. He wagged his tail, waiting for the snack. "Sit," Milla told him. Chip dropped his bottom to the ground and then quickly stood up again. Milla gave her pet a firm look and repeated the command. "Sit, Chip."

But Chip was too excited about the banana to follow directions. He nuzzled Milla's shirt with his snout, spreading a muddy splotch across the front of her first-day-of-school outfit. Milla laughed, even though she knew she wasn't supposed to do that when her pig was naughty. It was important to be firm and show him who was boss, but sometimes it was very hard to hold her giggles in.

Forcing herself to frown, Milla ordered the pig to sit *again*.

Chip oinked. He butted his head up against Milla's leg. He sat, wriggled, and then let out a loud grunt. Milla could tell he was trying to prove how badly he wanted the treat. Finally, he settled his bottom on the ground and waited patiently.

"Good boy." Milla kneeled and fed him half the banana. It was gone in seconds. Chip grunted again. "Don't beg," Milla scolded, handing him the other half. "It's not polite. If you must know, you really aren't acting much like a prince." In response, Chip climbed into Milla's lap and sat down. "Oof!"

The pig settled in for a cuddle, nosing Milla for more treats. "All right, stinker," Milla said, pushing his snout away. "We'll take a break from the story. Maybe tomorrow I'll set up a cardboard city and let you be the monster that destroys it. Would you like that role better?"

Milla flopped onto her back and gazed up

at the wispy clouds drifting by overhead. Chip rested his heavy head on her stomach. "Once upon a time," she whispered, starting a new story, "there was an adventurous young girl. This brave explorer—and her pet pig—set off on a journey to the ends of the earth."

Chocolate Chip huffed a sigh.

"Yeah, yeah, I know there are no *ends* of the earth," Milla muttered. "This is just make-believe. It's not like I'm about to set off on an adventure to some far-off place anyway. Let's pretend, okay?" She continued her story. "Milla the mighty explorer and her noble pet were on a quest. They wanted to hike the tallest mountains, dogsled to the North Pole, white-water raft in the wildest rivers, and explore crumbling old castles in distant lands."

Milla loved reading and writing about anything, but there was nothing she enjoyed more than creating adventures for herself. In Milla's stories, she was always a brave hero without fears or worries of any kind. One of the things Milla most loved about writing was that she was totally in charge and got to make all the decisions about what would happen on her adventures. The only limitation was her imagination, and her imagination was vast. "Milla was the greatest explorer who had ever lived. Nothing could stop her—"

"Hon!" Milla's mom, Erica, poked her head out the back door and called, "We need to leave in five minutes or you're going to be late for your first day of fifth grade." Chocolate Chip leaped up and raced toward the house. He usually got a treat when he came inside from the backyard.

"Coming," Milla said. She brushed at her shirt, trying to wipe away some of the pig slobber and mud. Too late—it was caked on, but Milla didn't mind. She made her way toward the house, whispering, "Nothing could stop this fearless explorer . . . except for the fact that she was still just a kid and she never went anywhere other than school and her own backyard. But someday!" Milla swung her lunch up and off the kitchen counter, swiped her backpack off its hook, and headed for the front door. "Someday—*soon*— Milla the brave, bold, capable explorer would set off on her own and conquer the world."

"You'll have to conquer the world next week," Milla's other mom, Eleanor—whom Milla called mum—said in her lilting British accent. "This week's adventure is fifth grade, and school waits for no one." She pointed to a pile of folded clothes on the arm of the couch. "Get dressed, love."

Milla glanced down at the dirty shirt and jeans she was wearing. "I'm already dressed." She tugged at her dark ponytail, tucked a loose curl behind one ear, and smiled.

Milla's parents stood side by side. Her mom folded her light, freckled arms across her chest, while her mum merely raised her eyebrows. Somehow, they were both always able to say a whole lot without saying a word.

"But I like this shirt," Milla told them.

"It's covered in snout snot," her mom said. "And mud."

"It's only a *little* mud. Me and Chip's adventures are messy." Milla grinned as she pulled off her soiled shirt. She knew it was pointless to argue with either of her parents. Sassing back never seemed to work out the way she wanted it to. She wriggled into a clean pair of jeans and the bright blue cactus T-shirt her mum had set out for her. Then she waved her arms in the air. "Ta-da! Better?"

"Much," her mum agreed, leaning in for a hug. Her dark curly hair tickled Milla's cheek. "Have a great first day. I might see you after my shift tonight, if you're still awake. Yeah?"

Milla squeezed her back, breathing in the familiar smell of her mum's lemony-fresh hand lotion. Because her mum was a nurse and often worked long shifts with weird hours, Milla didn't always get to see her first thing in the morning or last thing at night. Her mom worked slightly more regular hours as a vet and usually handled most of the school pickup and drop-off duties on her way to and from the clinic.

"Chop-chop," her mom said, jingling her keys and heading for the door.

Milla slung her bag over her shoulder, then bent down to give Chocolate Chip a hug. He smelled much *less* lemony-fresh but was still lovable in his own way. The pig pressed his snout against Milla's stomach, rubbing a wet splotch right across the front of her clean shirt. She pulled away, laughing as she raced out the front door. As she fled, she called back to her mum over her shoulder, "Too late to change again. Like you said, school adventures wait for no one!"

2
FiRSt-DAY SURPRiSES

The moment her mom dropped her off in front of Walter Roy Elementary, Milla's friend Piper Andelman shouted and waved to her from across the playground. "Milla! You have to try one of these." She ran over and held out a tiny coconut-crusted muffin. When Piper smiled, her eyes sparkled behind crooked glasses. Two messy reddish braids dangled out the bottom of a fleecy winter hat. All year round, even when they were living through the hottest months of summer, Piper liked having something on her head.

"You know I can't," Milla said apologetically.

Because of her food allergies, Milla never ate any food that she couldn't be sure was safe. She'd once eaten a cookie at a preschool potluck and it had sent her to the hospital. She'd been so sick that she couldn't even remember her ride in the ambulance. Her parents were constantly paranoid about her having another reaction, but Milla had been careful about what she ate for so long now that it was second nature. "Allergies, remember?"

"Totally, one-thousand-percent nut-free. No dairy, either," Piper promised, crossing a finger over her chest. "I wiped down the whole kitchen before I made them and triple-washed everything. I didn't want you to have to miss out." She wiggled the muffin in midair. "I'm calling them Fifth-Grade Flurries. Coconut, carrot, a touch of cinnamon, and one little secret ingredient— a new recipe. What do you think?"

Milla took a bite, feeling grateful that her friend was always willing to work around her allergies. Coconut, carrot, and cinnamon sounded slightly odd, but somehow almost everything Piper baked or cooked tasted amazing.

Piper was part scientist, part chef, and her inventions were usually delicious. She loved playing around in the kitchen, often combining weird ingredients to create unusual new treats. Of course, there had been more than a few failures over the years: once, she'd whipped up a strange fruit punch that fizzed and bubbled like a witch's brew and turned a very yucky brown color; another time, she'd made candy that was so sticky it had yanked a filling out of one of her back teeth.

Milla popped the rest of the muffin in her mouth, trying not to gobble it up as quickly as Chocolate Chip would eat one of his treats. "That's super yummy," she told her friend. "What's the secret ingredient?"

"Soda water! I need to adjust the amount to get a little more puff next time," Piper said. "They're too flat, but still acceptable."

Suddenly, Milla felt a tug on the side of her

jeans. She looked down and found Piper's little sister, Finley, gazing up at her. Finley was starting kindergarten, and Piper had been put in charge of delivering her sister from the playground to her classroom for the first few weeks of school.

"Baaaa," the little girl bleated.

"Hi, Finley," Milla said. "Are you excited for kindergarten?"

"Baaaa," Finley said again.

Piper rolled her eyes. "Ignore her. She's a

naughty little sheep. I thought I lost my first-day-of-school shirt this morning—but then I figured out that Finley had stolen it. She was trying to chew *holes* in my *shirt*! This little critter claims sheep love to eat clothing."

"She's a pretty cute critter, at least," Milla said, laughing as she followed Piper and her sister off the playground and through the school's front doors. "But, Finley, isn't it goats that eat weird stuff?"

"Whatever," Piper said. "Finley's not a sheep *or* a goat, so she shouldn't be eating anything unusual. Unless I cooked it." She gently guided her sister toward the kindergarten hallway. "Fin, where's your name badge?"

Finley blinked, but said nothing more than "Baaaa" again. All kindergarteners were supposed to wear a special name badge that identified them as school newbies the entire first week. "Baaaa!" Finley shouted one last time, then galloped into her classroom.

"Oh well," Piper said with a shrug. "She's the third Andelman to come through this school. They probably know who she is by now."

Milla and Piper made their way down the hall and stopped in front of one of the three fifth-grade classrooms. For the first time ever, the two girls would be in different homerooms this year. "Good luck," Milla said, holding her hand up for a high five. "Don't sit in the front row. I hear Mr. Mohan spits when he talks."

"I brought safety goggles, just in case," Piper joked, high-fiving her back. Then she pushed her glasses up the bridge of her nose and marched into the room. "See you at recess."

Milla slowly made her way toward her home-room. She had been assigned to Mr. Poloski's class. Though Milla knew most of the other fifth graders, she wasn't very good friends with anyone in her homeroom, so she was a little nervous. "It'll be an adventure," she whispered to herself. She hoped saying that would make it true.

As soon as everyone had found their assigned desks and Mr. Poloski had taken attendance, the fifth graders were called to the gym for a special meeting with the principal.

"An assembly on day one?" Ruby Fawcett whooped, pumping her fist in the air. "Yes!" The only things Milla knew about Ruby were that she had a twin brother and she was the best soccer player in fifth grade. Ruby sometimes missed school because her team played in tournaments in other states. Milla smiled at Ruby, who grinned back. Milla decided fifth grade was starting out pretty great—they'd never had special assemblies in fourth grade!

When they got to the gym, the school's principal, Ms. Burniac, called for attention. "Welcome to your last year at Walter Roy Elementary," she said. Ruby's twin brother, Henry, stood up and did a little dance. Everyone laughed, but Ms. Burniac looked unimpressed. "I hope, Mr. Fawcett, that the fifth graders will prove to be excellent role models for the younger students at our school this year." She paused, waiting for Henry and his friends to settle down.

"Okay, now that that's taken care of," Ms. Burniac continued. "I'm excited to announce that we are starting a new program for the fifth grade this year. To help prepare you for middle school and beyond, you'll each be assigned to an advisory group. Several times each week, you'll meet with a teacher mentor and small groups of your peers to set goals and plan for your futures. The groups will be led by our fifth-grade homeroom teachers and several of our specialist teachers."

Milla glanced over at the teachers lined up against one wall of the gym. The group of teacher-advisors included all three fifth-grade homeroom teachers, the art teacher, the school's media specialist, a math specialist, the PE teacher, and the assistant principal. Milla spotted one new face in the bunch—a woman wearing a knee-length black skirt over colorful striped tights, along with a bright green long-sleeve T-shirt. She wasn't super young, but she wasn't old, either—and the first thing Milla thought was that she didn't look like *any* of the other teachers at their school. Ms. Burniac introduced her as Ms. Bancroft, the new music teacher.

"We have split the class into groups that will be led by one of these teachers. As part of the advisory program," Ms. Burniac went on, "each of you will be asked to keep a journal throughout the year."

Piper, who had squeezed forward into an open spot beside Milla, groaned. Piper hated writing almost as much as Milla *loved* writing.

"You'll have your first meeting with your advisory team this afternoon," the principal went on. "Group lists will be posted after lunch."

Piper whispered to Milla, *"Please, please, please* let us be in the same group. Then you can write my journal entries for me."

Milla shook her head and smiled to herself.

She knew Piper was kidding—sort of.

"The other thing I wanted to discuss with all of you is our annual fifth-grade overnight." Someone whooped at the back of the crowd. Milla didn't need to look back to know it was Henry and his friends making a ruckus again. Ms. Burniac held up her hand and then said, "I'm sure most of you are already aware that the fifth graders kick off the school year with an overnight adventure trip. In just a few weeks, you'll all be braving a high-ropes course, learning to navigate your way through the wilderness *without* help from a cell phone GPS app, canoeing, and much more."

There was an excited murmur as everyone began talking about the overnight. Ms. Burniac cleared her throat, then added, "Your advisory groups will also be your activity groups at Adventure Camp. The overnight will be an excellent opportunity for the groups to bond. Homeroom teachers will be sending permission slips home today. They're due back in two weeks, so be sure to get them signed quickly."

The gym was buzzing as all the fifth graders lined up to return to their classrooms. "Fingers crossed that they put us together," Piper said, squeezing Milla's arm before stepping aside to join her class line. "Then we'll be in the same activity group for the overnight, too!"

Milla nodded. She really wanted to get swept up in everyone's excitement. The fifth-grade overnight was sure to be an amazing adventure. The only problem was that her parents tended to be overprotective, and she was worried what they would say about her going on an overnight field trip. Milla had never even had a sleepover at a friend's house before. A night away from home was a *big* deal—for her *and* her moms.

Though she desperately wanted to go on the trip with her classmates, Milla had a sinking suspicion this was one big adventure she was probably going to have to miss out on.

Milla

❀ ~~Once upon a time, there was a fifth-grade girl who loved to explore.~~

Once upon a time, there was a fifth-grade girl who loved the <u>idea</u> of exploring. But this poor thing had never actually gone on any kind of real adventure. In fact, she had never really been <u>anywhere</u> except her little town. (Okay, there was the one time she visited relatives in Ohio and got to go to a waterpark. And that other time she spent two nights in Florida because of her mom's work trip. But she wasn't even allowed to go out past her knees in the ocean, so it really doesn't count!)

Ever since she could remember, this brave girl had been keeping a growing list of places she hoped she might get to visit someday. There were castles to explore, mountains to climb, and so many types of food to taste (all nut- and dairy-free, of course).

But so far, the only <u>big</u> adventures this girl has had are the ones she's read or written about in stories. Is that fair? Does anyone believe that made-up adventures are as fun as real ones? No. Everyone knows they're not.

3
THE MAGICAL CLASSROOM

"Have you found your name yet?" Milla asked Piper, craning her neck to get a glimpse at the advisory group lists. Lunch had just ended, and the fifth-grade hallway was a tangle of voices and bodies. Everyone was searching the lists for their own name, as well as their friends' names.

"Neither of us is in Mr. Hulsey's or Ms. Ling's group," Piper said loudly. She stood on tiptoe and squinted at the lists. "I don't think we're on Mr. Pederson's list, either."

Milla couldn't get close enough to the wall to read any names. It didn't help that Mariana Sanchez was standing right in front of her, and she was one of the tallest kids in their grade by far. Suddenly, Mari spun around and smiled, "Milla, it looks like we're in the same group. You're in our group, too, Piper. I guess I'll see you guys this afternoon." She gave them both a thumbs-up and loped away.

Milla and Piper stepped forward to study the list. "We're in Ms. Bancroft's group," Milla read. "That's the new music teacher, right?"

"Yeah," Piper said. "She looks nice enough." She pressed her finger to the paper and read off the other names in the group: "Milla Bannister-Cook—that's you; Piper Andelman—*moi*, obviously; Mariana Sanchez; Ruby Fawcett; and Zahra Sharif. I guess they went easy on the new teacher. Most of the groups have eight or nine kids, and there are only five of us. Best of all, no boys. Phew."

Milla nodded. She was happy to discover she knew everyone in her group a little bit—at least, enough to know they were all super nice. Ruby and Mariana were both really sporty. But while Ruby was loud and outspoken, Mari was quiet and kept to herself most of the time. Milla had never been in class with Zahra, but everyone knew she was the best artist in their grade. She had even won some sort of big prize last year. She'd been on the news and everything. The only other thing Milla knew about Zahra was that she wore a colorful headscarf every day, along with really interesting clothes that looked hand-sewn and Zahra-designed. Nothing like Milla's own boring T-shirts and jeans.

"I'm excited," Milla told Piper. "Our group looks good."

Piper said, "And this means we'll be together for Adventure Camp!"

Milla half smiled. She wanted to share her friend's excitement. But once again, there was that niggling worry that her moms wouldn't let her join the rest of the fifth-grade class on the overnight. It wasn't that Milla's parents were mean, or super strict, or trying to punish her for something; they just worried about her. And even Milla had to admit, they worried for good reasons.

First, there were the food allergies. When she was little, Milla's parents had always monitored every morsel of food that came near her. But then, that one time, they had gotten caught up in conversation at the preschool potluck and it had led to Milla's horrible allergic reaction and the scary trip in the ambulance. Since then, they'd watched her like a hawk and were very cautious about where she went and with whom. As she'd gotten older, Milla had learned to be really careful about food herself—but she knew her moms still worried every day, because you just never know what might happen.

And then there was the scar to remind her of the *other* reason her moms hovered over her. Milla ran her thumb across her cheek, feeling the raised jagged line that ran from below her eye to her jawline. Just a few days before Milla's fifth birthday, her family had met up with some friends at a neighborhood park. The kids were all playing on one side of the park while the adults watched from benches on the other.

The dog came out of nowhere. No one ever figured out what had provoked it to bite a kid. But for some reason, Milla had been bitten—badly—and Milla's parents had never forgiven themselves. Even though it wasn't their fault, they blamed themselves for not being close enough to prevent it from happening. She was fine now, and they always thanked their lucky stars everything had turned out as well as it did. But her moms said the scar was there to help them remember she needed their protection. They loved to remind her that she was their one and only child and it was their sacred duty to keep her safe.

"Yoo-hoo," Piper said, putting her face close to Milla's. She gently bonked her forehead against her friend's. "Hellooo. You in there?"

Milla nodded. "Yeah, sorry—" Before she could say more, the teachers called all the fifth graders into their classrooms. Milla replied over her shoulder, "See ya at the meeting!"

"Welcome!" Ms. Bancroft said later that day, waving Milla and the others into her classroom for their first advisory group meeting. "Please come in and make yourselves at home. I'm Ms. Bancroft. You may call me Ms. Bancroft, Ms. B, Amy, Hey You . . . frankly, I'm not big on formality." Piper and Mariana lingered silently in the doorway, but Ms. Bancroft ushered them in. "Come on, no need to be shy."

Milla let her gaze wander around the classroom. Before Mr. Fairbanks had retired, the music room had been boring beige with old posters hanging on the walls and a collection of instruments resting on shelves. Now the walls were jam-packed with printouts of colorful quotes, pictures of fairy-tale princesses and famous musicians, lyrics from songs, and magazine cutouts of everything from colorful flowers and elaborate cakes to musical instruments and fancy shoes.

"Whoa, this room looks seriously different," Ruby announced.

"A bit, yes." Ms. Bancroft laughed. Her laugh was low and rumbling and made her whole face light up. She had a wide, welcoming smile, and something about her immediately made Milla feel relaxed and cheerful. "I love being surrounded by some of my favorite things. There's nothing sadder than a boring white classroom." Ms. Bancroft put her hands on her hips. "What do you think? Do you like what I've done with the place?"

Milla nodded. She really, really loved it. She wondered what her parents would do if she decorated her bedroom like this. Ms. Bancroft's room

was so colorful and vibrant and *personal*.

"I see smiles, so I'm going to take that as a yes," Ms. Bancroft said. "Feel free to look around—exploring my classroom will help you get to know me a little better."

Milla wandered through the room, trying to take it all in. Brightly colored quotes swirled around walls. Words and advice exploded out of every nook and corner. The piano had been covered with the words "'Believe you can and you're halfway there.' —Theodore Roosevelt."

In the far corner of the room was a picture of Belle from *Beauty and the Beast* on beautiful textured paper. At the top it said "'I want adventure in the great wide somewhere!' —Belle." Milla grinned; she definitely agreed with that sentiment!

On the other side of the room was a black-and-white photo of the Dalai Lama, above a banner that read "Happiness is not ready-made. It comes from your own actions."

Marching across the window were the words "'Let us make our future now, and let us make our dreams tomorrow's reality.' —Malala Yousafzai."

While the five girls looked around, Ms. Bancroft handed out plain blue notebooks. "These are the journals Ms. Burniac mentioned this morning," she explained. "I'll be giving you all some writing prompts throughout the year—assignments that should be fun, but that will also help us get to know each other better."

She passed a notebook to Milla, adding, "I'd love to see each of you decorate your journal in your own personal style. A plain blue notebook is pretty uninspiring. Turn your notebook into something that feels unique and special. I want your journal to reflect *you*—just like my classroom reflects *me*."

Milla already knew exactly how she would decorate her journal. A picture of Chocolate Chip would go front and center, of course. And she would cover the rest with pictures of the Taj Mahal, Mount Rainier, sled dogs, Norwegian fjords, and other places and things she'd like to explore. That would definitely be inspiring!

"Your classroom reminds me of an artist's canvas," Zahra said. She ran her hand across one wall, stopping in front of a picture of Cinderella. A speech bubble next to the princess's head said "'If you keep on believing, the dreams that you wish will come true.'" Zahra read it aloud and then spun around. "I like this quote, but . . ."

Ms. Bancroft cocked her head to one side. "But . . . ? Feel free to speak your mind in here. Differences of opinion are always welcome."

Zahra shrugged. "I know it's important to keep believing and wishing . . . but I think it's just as important to work hard. Wishes only get you so far, right?"

Ms. Bancroft raised her eyebrows. "That is a very good point," she said with a wink. "What's your name?"

"Zahra Sharif," she said.

"It's lovely to meet you, Zahra," Ms. Bancroft said. She clapped once, for attention, and said, "Why don't we each pull a chair into the center of the room and take care of introductions. I'm guessing you all know each other's names, but I'm new here and need to start with the basics. How's that sound?"

There was a chorus of "Okays" and "Goods."

Once they were all seated, Ms. Bancroft said, "I'll begin by saying that I'm so excited to be a part of this group. We'll be getting together a couple of times each week, all year long. There's no set plan for what *should* happen at our meetings, but my hope is that you'll all feel this is a safe space to talk through any issues or challenges you're facing—at school or at home. I'd also love to spend some time talking about your hopes and dreams for the future."

Ms. Bancroft looked around the circle, stopping to give each of them a warm smile. "I bet you all have big dreams and wishes for your future, am I right?" No one answered, but Ms. Bancroft didn't seem discouraged. She charged on, adding, "This year, my only requirement in this group is that each of you dare to dream big! I hope you'll allow me to be your guide while you begin to steer your own ships toward the future."

When Ms. Bancroft said the thing about ships, Ruby snorted, as though she was trying to hold back a laugh. But Milla was pretty sure she was the only one who heard. Milla glanced over at Piper and got the impression she, too, was trying to hold back some giggles. But like Milla, both Mariana and Zahra seemed very interested in what Ms. Bancroft was saying.

"Let's jump right in," Ms. Bancroft said. "I'd love for each of you to introduce yourself and share one of your big dreams."

Milla's eyes widened. That was a *big* thing to ask! She hated being put on the spot and really didn't like to talk about herself. Milla never even let anyone read the stories she'd written, since they felt too private and personal. And now she was expected to blurt out a big dream in front of four of her classmates, three of whom she didn't even know that well?

Milla looked around the circle. Zahra and Mari were both looking down at their laps. Piper shot Milla a funny, nervous look. It seemed no one knew what to say.

Just before the silence started to feel uncomfortable, Ruby loudly announced, "Hey, I'm Ruby Fawcett and my big dream is to someday be in the Olympics. Probably as a member of the US Women's Soccer team, but I'm open to other sports, too. But me competing in the Olympics is *not* just a dream—it's a fact." The way she said this made everyone laugh. Ruby smiled and then raised her eyebrows, daring anyone to question her.

"That's a great dream, Ruby," Ms. Bancroft said. "I love your confidence. I'm looking forward to getting to know you this year." She turned to the others and asked, "Who'd like to go next?" When no one else spoke up, Ms. Bancroft stood and walked across the circle. She stood right in front of Milla and reached out to shake her hand. "Hi there. What's your name?"

"Um . . . Milla?" Milla said quietly. She shook Ms. Bancroft's hand. It was warm and rough. Something about the handshake made Milla feel good—like she was a person with ideas that mattered. "Milla Bannister-Cook."

"Hello, Milla. It's pronounced Milla, like vanilla, correct? Not Mee-la?" Milla nodded. Many people mispronounced her name. She really appreciated that Ms. Bancroft had asked! "Tell us something about yourself, Milla. What's one of your big dreams?"

Milla felt the whole group looking at her. She nervously touched her scar, wondering if they were all looking at it. Sometimes people stared at her scar in a way that made her feel icky. Once, a little boy at the grocery store had pointed at her and announced that her face looked broken. In second grade, one of her classmates had cruelly told her she reminded him of the Beast in *Beauty and the Beast*. "I love to write," Milla said finally. "I would love to be an author someday."

Ms. Bancroft smiled warmly. "Wonderful! What do you write?"

"Adventure stories, mostly," Milla said, trying to shake off her nerves. "I would love to be an explorer and write stories inspired by my travels and adventures."

Ms. Bancroft clapped. "I love it. That's an excellent dream, Milla. Who wants to go next?"

Milla breathed a sigh of relief. She'd impressed Ms. Bancroft. Now it was someone else's turn in the spotlight.

"My name is Piper Andelman," Piper said, pushing her glasses up her nose. "I love food science and building my own recipes. One thing I would love to do is enter a cooking competition on TV. I'd like to learn how they make astronaut food, too, and help create some new recipes for the space program. I also hope to invent something that actually keeps fruit from spoiling and cookies from going stale." She shrugged. "That's not everything I want to do, but those are a few dreams I have."

Ms. Bancroft said, "I'm eager to hear more, Piper. Sounds like you're going to have your plate full. Thank you."

"I'm Zahra Sharif," Zahra said, waving at everyone. "I love making art and would one day love to see something I created in a museum or on display somewhere important."

"Did you do the henna art on your hands?" Ms. Bancroft said, pointing to the reddish-brown swirls that swooped across Zahra's hands and wrists. "It's lovely."

"Yes," Zahra said. "My cousin got married last weekend, so we all did henna for the party."

Finally, it was Mariana's turn. "I'm Mariana

Sanchez—you can call me Mari or Mariana, I like them both. I come from a family of swimmers, and I guess . . ." She broke off, then glanced at Ruby. With a slight shrug, Mariana continued. "I guess maybe I'd like to swim at Olympic trials someday, like my mom and older sister both did?" She tucked a loose strand of dark hair behind her ear and quietly added, "But honestly, I'm not sure that's my big dream. I guess I haven't really figured out what I want to do with my life yet. I'm still deciding. I'm sorry."

Ms. Bancroft nodded. "No need to apologize. I appreciate your honesty, Mariana. It took me a long time to figure out what I wanted to do with my life," she said. Then she laughed. "The truth is, I'm *still* figuring it out. You don't need to know anything for sure. All I ask is that you let yourselves dream big. I want to help you make some of your wishes come true. We're a team, and we'll work together to support one another."

She smiled warmly. "Now, during our last

few minutes together, I'd like to discuss the first journal assignment." Ms. Bancroft swept her arm around the room, stopping to point at a picture of Cinderella, then Belle, then Ariel, then Jasmine.

"You may have noticed that I have a thing for princesses," she said. "Always have, always will. I bet I watched both *Sleeping Beauty* and *Snow White* three hundred times as a kid. I spent *hours* wishing I could live out in the middle of the woods like those two young princesses did. There was something about their stories that helped me begin to figure out what kind of woman I wanted to become." Ms. Bancroft stood up and rested her hands on the back of her chair. "Because princesses helped me find *my* big dream, I'd like to bring princesses into your first writing assignment: I want each of you to think of a princess you connect with or feel inspired by and explain why. Dig deep and really think about your answer. Got it?"

Everyone nodded. The bell rang then, signaling an end to the first day of fifth grade. "I'll see you on Friday!" Ms. Bancroft said, waving. They all stood up to leave. But as Piper stuffed her journal deep inside her backpack, she looked at the other girls and asked, "Do you guys think we should come up with a name for our group? Something other than Ms. Bancroft's advisory?"

"Ooh," Mariana said. "That's a good idea."

"Can we call ourselves a club?" Ruby asked. "My brother will get seriously jealous if I'm in a club he isn't a part of."

"I like the idea of this being a club of sorts," Ms. Bancroft said with a wink. "Our meetings will feel more personal that way."

"The Wish Club?" Milla suggested.

"Wishes and Dreams Club?" Zahra said.

"Club Dream Come True?" Mari offered.

"What about the Daring Dreamers Club?" Piper said. "Ms. Bancroft keeps telling us we should dare to dream big. . . ."

"That's perfect," Milla said.

"I love it," Zahra agreed.

Milla waved at the other girls and their advisor as she tucked her journal under her arm and headed out to her locker. "Have some fun with this first assignment," Ms. Bancroft called after them. "See you for our next club meeting later this week, Daring Dreamers!"

4
PERMiSSiON SLiP
PROBLEMS

The moment Milla got home from school, Chocolate Chip scampered off his bed in the corner of the living room and greeted her with a chorus of grunts and groans. He wiggled his body and wagged his little tail, snorting and snuffling excitedly.

"Looks like someone missed you today," Milla's mom said, tossing her keys on the table by the door. "Make sure you feed him, okay?"

"I'm on it," Milla promised.

"Hiya, Chip!" Piper said, bending down to greet the pig. Piper and Milla had made plans to hang out after school while Piper's dad took Finley on a dad date. A one-on-one ice cream date after the first day of kindergarten was one of many Andelman family traditions. "I think you've gotten even bigger since the last time I saw you, bud. You're not such a mini pig anymore."

Milla laughed as Chip thumped against Piper's leg, nearly knocking her over. "'Mini' is kind of a running joke now," she told her friend. "He's forty-five pounds and still growing!"

"He doesn't look that heavy," Piper noted.

"Pigs carry their weight differently from dogs," Milla told her. She'd had to learn a lot about pigs, *fast,* after her family adopted Chip from a couple who couldn't take care of him anymore. The breeder who sold Chip had said he was a "teacup pig," but Milla now knew there really was no such thing. When Chip kept growing—passing twenty, then thirty pounds—his original owners had realized they were in way over their heads. Milla's mom had agreed to adopt him from them. She had been trained as a large-animal vet, so she knew what a huge responsibility pigs could be and how to care for them. "Want to feed him a snack?"

Piper whooped. "Yes, please!"

Milla got a couple of carrots out of the fridge and passed them to her friend. Chip crunched and munched while Milla and Piper chatted about the first day of school.

"Ms. Bancroft seems super cool," Piper said slowly. "But also a little odd . . ."

"That's what I like about her," Milla said. "She seems really interesting. And I think it's great that she's so excited about the advisory program."

"Ahem, I think you mean the *Daring Dreamers Club*?" Piper corrected her.

"Right," Milla said, nodding.

Suddenly, in a silly voice that sounded nothing like Ms. Bancroft's, Piper waved her arms in the air and crooned, "You all have unique and special futures. I am here to help you figure out how to make all your wishes come true!" She giggled, and then said, "I mean this in a good way, but there were a few times today when Ms. B sounded a little like one of my grandma's inspirational birthday cards."

Milla laughed. "She's obviously very supportive. All that stuff she said about helping us steer our ships toward the future and pursuing our dreams? It was really sweet. A little cheesy, but sweet." Milla pulled the new blue journal out of her backpack and flipped through the blank pages. "You know what I'm excited about? That she's letting us decorate our journals."

"Me too. Honestly, that's the *only* part of the journal I'm excited about." Piper stood up and followed Milla to her bedroom. Chip trailed along after them, eager to go wherever the action was. "Her classroom is seriously amazing. I didn't even know teachers were *allowed* to do that."

"I know!" Milla said. "I wonder if they *are*

allowed. . . . Ms. Bancroft doesn't seem like the kind of person who would worry that much about the school's decorating rules. I get the impression she's kind of a rebel."

Piper settled on Milla's bedroom floor, pulling her knees up under her chin. "Total rebel. She's definitely going to be a fun group leader during the overnight."

"For sure," Milla said, grinning.

"Did you remember to bring your permission slip home?" Piper asked, pawing through her backpack. She groaned and muttered, "I think I already lost mine. I swear I put it in my bag, but . . ." Milla laughed. Piper was always losing stuff—it was part of her charm. "I'll have to ask Mr. Mohan for a new one tomorrow."

Milla pulled her own permission slip out of her backpack. She'd been hoping she might have the chance to talk to her moms about the trip right away, that night. But then she remembered her mum was working late, and she knew her mom wouldn't sign anything without having the chance to discuss it as a family first.

Piper kneeled down on the floor and rummaged through Milla's stacks of books. "Chip's not the only thing that's grown since the last time I was over here," she said. "Your house is going to collapse under the weight of all these books!"

Several years ago, Milla's library had outgrown the shelves in her bedroom. Now she kept piles of fiction against the wall near her closet, nonfiction survival stories in her bottom dresser drawer, and mountains of travel books stacked under her bed. The adventure stories she had written over the years were in a tall pile on her desk. "I love reading. And books are the only way I can get out and explore other parts of the world."

Piper pushed her glasses up and said, "I guess you already know what you're going to write about for Ms. B's first journal assignment, then, huh? Your princess is easy—you're totally Belle."

Milla frowned. "I guess that's sort of true. We both love to read. And she wants to escape her tiny town." She paused. "But sometimes I feel a little like Rapunzel, too. I'm trapped in my messy room reading about the world outside, but I've never really been allowed to go anywhere other than my own backyard. I love that Rapunzel escapes and sets out on an adventure."

"Yeesh," Piper said, making a shocked face.

"So are you saying your moms are like Mother Gothel? That's kind of harsh."

Milla laughed. "I wasn't thinking of it like that! My parents are definitely *not* like Mother Gothel, you're right. So yeah, I guess maybe Belle is better?"

"Whoa whoa *whoa*," Piper said, waving her hands around. "I just realized something major. You have a *teacup* pig named Chip—just like little Chip the teacup in the movie! You are totally Belle!" She stood up and spun circles around the room as she sang, *"She wants adventure in the great wide somewhere—"* Piper broke off, grinning. "I know the lines to pretty much every Disney movie ever made. They're on nonstop at my house."

There was something about Piper's singing and dancing that got Chip all riled up. The silly pig started running circles around Milla's bedroom, knocking things off shelves. He burrowed his snout under a pillow that had fallen off her bed. Then he started pushing stuffed animals around the room. That made Piper laugh and sing even louder. She finally stopped when Chip overturned a pile of books and spilled a whole box of markers on the floor.

Once Milla got Chip settled down, she pulled out a bunch of *National Geographic* magazines and scissors and colored pencils. She and Piper continued to chat about Ms. Bancroft's princess assignment while they worked on decorating their journals.

By the time Piper left an hour later, both girls had written their first journal entries and had gotten a good start on decorating their notebooks. The front of Piper's was filled with cutout magazine pictures of some of her favorite foods, and she'd drawn a set of beakers and a colorful strand of DNA using metallic markers. Milla's was covered with photos of places she wanted to visit—including a picture of the high-ropes course at Adventure Camp that she'd printed off the internet.

Looking at that picture made Milla think about her permission slip again. She wanted to go on the trip, more than anything. She *had* to go. The question was, how could she be sure her moms would say yes? Milla had never spent a night away from her parents before—ever. The only time she'd had sleepovers with friends, they had stayed at her house. But Milla was ready for this. At least, she hoped she was.

Milla knew her moms would have a lot of questions about camp food, the chaperones, and all the activities and safety equipment. So she opened up the shared family laptop and started to poke around on the Adventure Camp website again. She hoped it might convince them to say yes if she'd done some research and was able to answer any questions they had. She wanted to make sure they felt confident that she could take care of herself!

Milla decided to write her parents a letter outlining some of the reasons why they should let her go. She had always found it easier to express her feelings in writing. When the letter was ready, she rolled it up with her permission slip and tied both papers to Chocolate Chip's collar. Who could resist a pig messenger?

"Go, Chip," Milla said, pushing him toward the living room. "Be off, my noble piggy messenger, and deliver this to Mom!"

Chip trotted away. Milla counted to twenty, then followed. But when she walked out of her bedroom, she discovered that Chip hadn't made it very far. He'd stopped just down the hallway, where he was lying on the floor . . . munching happily on the remains of both papers. Her naughty pig had somehow slipped the message off his neck and totally destroyed it.

Milla groaned. So much for that plan. It looked like Piper wouldn't be the only one asking for a new permission slip!

Piper

Assignment: Think of a princess you connect
with or feel inspired by and explain why (one
page).

Here's something you should know about me,
Ms. Bancroft: I don't like to write. I really
don't do journals. But since this is something I
have to do, I'll try. Luckily, we watch a lot of
Disney Princess movies at my house. My little
sister, Finley, is obsessed. Her favorite movie is
Snow White, because she likes the songs and
the Dwarfs. She also really likes Brave,
because she thinks Merida's little brothers
are hilarious.

But you didn't ask about Finley, did you?
This is supposed to be my assignment. Oh,
look! I almost filled up a page already.

Yay, me.

I guess now that you know about my passion

for food, my favorite princess movie is probably pretty obvious: <u>The Princess and the Frog.</u> I've always liked Tiana. She and I both love to cook, and like Tiana, I hope to run my own business someday. (I have an older brother, and I <u>really</u> hate being bossed around.) One other thing you should know about me is that using food for science is one of my favorite activities!

I love inventing new recipes, and I like seeing how adding different amounts of an ingredient or adjusting temperatures can change how something turns out. I also love coming up with experiments to test on foods we buy from the store. Someday I hope to be a great inventor and food scientist.

Well, that's more than a page. Phew!

5
ADVENTURE CAMP PLANNING

"How did your first assignment go?" Ms. Bancroft asked on Friday at the next meeting of the Daring Dreamers Club. For the first few months of school, each advisory group would be meeting two times per week, usually on Tuesdays and Fridays right at the end of the school day. "Would anyone be willing to share a snippet of your first journal entry?"

"I guess I'll go first. I wrote about Belle," Milla said, glancing at the picture of Belle on the music room wall. "We're similar because we both love to read and want to explore the world."

"That's great, Milla!" Ms. Bancroft said with a big smile. "What about the rest of you? Would anyone else be willing to read aloud some of what you wrote so we can get to know each other better?"

Milla and Zahra exchanged a quick look, and then both glanced down. Milla didn't like reading her writing aloud, and she wondered if Zahra felt the same. As Zahra hugged her journal tight against her chest, Milla could see that the blue notebook had been covered in elaborate flowers made of puff paint. There were similar painted flowers on Zahra's jeans that matched the colors in her headscarf. She looked like a walking piece of art.

After a long silence, Piper raised her hand. She read a few lines of her first journal entry aloud, nervously stumbling over the words a few times.

When she'd finished, Ms. Bancroft patted her on the shoulder. "Wonderful, Piper. I'm eager to read the rest of your entry. I feel these journals will be such a nice way for me to get to know all of you on a more personal level."

Mariana cleared her throat. "Um, Ms. Bancroft? Will you be collecting our journals today?"

"I'd planned to," Ms. Bancroft said with a frown. "I'll return them to you first thing Monday."

Mariana ran her fingers through her choppy hair. "I haven't had time to do the assignment yet. But I've been thinking about it a lot."

"I haven't finished, either," Ruby said. "I've got to be honest, Ms. B. I'm not a princess kind of girl."

Ms. Bancroft laughed. "I'm not expecting any of you to *be* a princess—I'm just asking you to use a Disney Princess for inspiration. Sometimes, welcoming new ideas and looking outside your comfort zone can help you think about things in ways that lead to fun surprises."

"I'll do my best," Ruby promised.

"That's all I ask," Ms. Bancroft said kindly.

"Now, let's switch gears. Since the first big activity we'll experience together as a group is the fifth-grade overnight trip, perhaps we should talk about it? What are some of the things you're most looking forward to at Adventure Camp?"

Ruby blurted out, "I'm hoping to kick my brother's butt during the girls versus guys soccer competition."

Ms. Bancroft nodded. "All right. I'll have to brush up on my dribbling skills."

"Oh," Ruby said, looking sheepish. "Teachers don't usually play." Then she added quickly, "But you're welcome to join the girls' team, Ms. B. If you want to."

"That's very kind of you, Ruby. I'll let you know." She laughed, then turned to the others. "Anyone else?"

"I heard the food is really good," Piper said. "My older brother went on this trip a few years ago, and he said that the breakfast is amazing."

"Good to know," Ms. Bancroft said.

Zahra hugged her knees to her chest and said, "I'm looking forward to getting out into the woods. I love being surrounded by all the colors in nature—birds, trees, flowers, water. Also, I've never been in a canoe. I can't wait to try it."

"Canoeing is super fun," Mariana told Zahra. "I bet you'll love it." Then she said, "My older sisters told me we all get to perform campfire skits, so that's probably what I'm most excited about." Milla glanced up, surprised. Mariana always seemed shy, so this answer surprised her. "Also, I think the high-ropes course sounds like it could be fun. The only thing is, I'm afraid of heights—I always get really shaky on bridges and when looking out the windows of high buildings, so I'm a little nervous I could freeze up."

"At least you'll be harnessed in," Milla told her. Mariana responded with a grateful smile. "It's very safe."

"What about you, Milla?" Ms. B prompted. "What are you most looking forward to?"

Milla swallowed. She still hadn't had time to talk with her parents about the trip. Her mum had been scheduled for night shifts all that week, so they hadn't sat down for dinner as a family since before school had started. And her mom was on call at the vet clinic that weekend—which meant things would be extra crazy and chaotic. Milla had briefly showed her new, unchewed permission slip to her mom after school on Wednesday, just to start the conversation. But as soon as they started talking, her mom got called into the clinic to figure out if some kid's favorite stuffed bunny was inside the family dog's stomach.

"I'm not sure I'm going," Milla admitted quietly.

Ms. Bancroft looked surprised. "Why is that?"

"Um," Milla began. "My parents are really protective, and I think they're going to be worried about sending me so far away for a whole night without them around to keep an eye on me."

"Have they considered volunteering to chaperone?" asked Ms. Bancroft. "There are still a few spots available."

"They both have to work," Milla said. What she *didn't* say was that she also wanted to prove to her parents—and herself—that she would be okay without their constant supervision. Of course, it would be fun to have one of them come along on the trip. Both her parents were really adventurous and would make great chaperones. But deep down, there was a piece of Milla that felt this could be the perfect chance to show her moms she could take care of herself, to prove to them that she was growing up. "I'm not sure they'll let me go without them. I have really bad food allergies, and they worry a lot about me getting hurt."

The other four girls were looking at her, but Milla couldn't meet their eyes. It was embarrassing to admit everything aloud. She had a feeling they were all looking at her scar, wondering whether all this stuff about her parents had something to do with the mark on her face. Even though she had never talked about how she'd gotten the scar with her classmates, she suddenly felt as if she should tell the group what had happened. Once it was out in the open, maybe she wouldn't feel as self-conscious about it. They were a club, after all. "I got bit by a dog when I was little," Milla explained, her hand reaching toward her face. "That's how I got this scar, and it's one of the other reasons my parents have always kept an extra-close eye on me."

"That makes sense," Ms. Bancroft said. "It must have been a scary time for all of you."

"I don't remember much about the day I got bit," Milla said. "They gave me some kind of medicine in the ambulance that helped me forget, and they kept me sedated for a few days afterward to make it easier for my body to heal." She ran her thumb over the raised line on her cheek. "But this scar is there to remind us all."

"I definitely get that," Ruby said, her voice cutting through what felt like minutes of silence. "But that happened a long time ago, right? Maybe you should find some way to show your parents that you're ready to go on a trip like this."

Piper chimed in, "You're very responsible, Milla. What if you were able to prove to them you know how to handle yourself in the world without them always watching out for you?"

"How would I prove that?" Milla asked. She loved the idea, but she wasn't sure how to act on it. Before she could say anything more, the rest of the Daring Dreamers Club began to brainstorm.

"Babysitting?" Mari suggested. "Or maybe pet-sitting?"

"Cleaning your room without being asked," Zahra added. "Or doing your own laundry."

"Making your own lunches for school?" Ruby suggested. "Clearing the table?"

Piper chimed in, "You could make dinner for your family!"

Throughout the rest of the meeting, the Daring Dreamers Club brainstormed dozens of ways that Milla could prove she was responsible and self-sufficient. By the end of the day, Milla had a plan in place . . . and she felt very hopeful that she would also have a signed permission slip in hand very soon!

6
PiG On tHe LOOSe

"Hey, Mom?" Milla said, looking up from her book. She had spent most of Friday night reading nonfiction stories about wilderness rangers who had escaped near-death situations. Even though she knew the fifth graders weren't likely to be in any life-threatening situations during their Adventure Camp trip, she figured it never hurt to be prepared—just in case. Chocolate Chip was curled up in a fuzzy blanket next to her, snuffling softly in his sleep. Milla rubbed his silky ear between two of her fingers and Chip groaned. "Can I talk to you about something?"

Milla's mom had just put her laptop away for the night, which was usually a good time to try to talk with her. "Is this about the field trip?" her mom asked, mid-yawn. She rubbed her eyes with her fists. "I'm exhausted and I've got a long weekend at work ahead of me, so now's really not the best time."

"Um, no?" Milla lied. She had been considering asking her mom if they could figure out when *would* be a good time to talk about the overnight. But based on her mom's reaction, she decided to skip that conversation for now and focus on her other plan—the one that would prove to her parents how responsible she was and make it impossible for them to say no to signing the permission slip. "I actually wanted to talk to you about show-and-tell at school."

"They still do show-and-tell in fifth grade?" her mom asked, pulling her eyebrows together. "What kinds of things do people present?"

"Most people share stories about their

weekends, or talk about something strange or funny that happened at home, or they show pictures from family trips," Milla said. Mr. Poloski didn't actually call it show-and-tell—he called it morning meeting. Since Milla didn't like to read the stories she wrote aloud, she never had much to tell. But now, thanks to the Daring Dreamers Club's suggestions, she'd finally come up with a really good idea of something she could share that would also prove how responsible she was. "I was wondering," she began, "if you would be willing to let me take Chocolate Chip to school to introduce him to my class."

Milla's mom closed her eyes and shook her head. "That doesn't seem like a good idea."

"Actually, I disagree," Milla said, trying to sound confident and mature. "Whenever I tell people at school that I have a pig, they think it sounds like so much fun. Chip *is* fun, but you and Mum and I all know that having a pig is *not* easy. I thought it would be helpful if I gave a talk on rescue animals, and how important it is to do your research before bringing a pet home."

For a long moment, Milla's mom didn't say anything. But then she smiled, and began to nod. "Honey, I think that's actually a really nice idea."

"Really?" Milla couldn't believe it. Her mom trusted her enough to let her take her pig to school! Now she just had to prove she could take care of him during his school visit, and then there was no *way* her parents would doubt that she could take care of *herself* on the overnight.

"Really. I'll email your teacher and see if he'd be willing to host a special guest." Her mom patted Chip's backside, and the snoozing pig let out a relaxed sigh. "Of course, I'll want to come along and help out. Just in case."

"Oh," Milla said, deflated. "Yeah, of course."

"But I'll let you do all the talking," her mom said, rubbing Milla's cheek. "Promise. This is your presentation. I trust you, kiddo."

That was all Milla needed to hear!

By the next Wednesday, everything was ready for Chip's elementary school debut. Just a few minutes after school started, Milla and her mom unloaded Chip from his travel kennel in the back of the car and clipped a leash onto his harness to lead him inside the building. Milla had suggested they wait for the crowd of kids to clear off the playground, because sometimes, big groups of people made Chip nervous.

Even though it was quiet on the school lawn when they got him out of the car, Chip seemed more excited than usual. He was so filled with energy that Milla had a hard time keeping hold of his leash. But she had a small plastic bag full of treats in her sweatshirt pocket. She hoped the promise of treats would keep her pig from misbehaving at school. "Chip," she said firmly, just as they approached the front door. "Wait."

The pig looked up at her, waving his snout in

the air. Milla grinned down at him. "Ready?" She offered Chip a chunk of sweet potato, then stepped through the door. "Let's do this, partner."

Milla felt nervous as they approached her classroom. She wanted so badly to prove to her mom that she could be responsible. She couldn't wait to show how much research she had done to prepare for the presentation! With her mom a few steps behind, Milla led Chip into the room, keeping him close by her side to help him stay relaxed. Everyone was sitting at their desks when they arrived, but a bunch of people gasped when they saw the pig, and a few kids shrieked and oohed. Mr. Poloski helpfully reminded everyone to stay seated and remain calm. Milla's mom settled in at the back of the classroom, politely staying out of the way.

"This is Chocolate Chip," Milla told her class. "Chip, sit." Chip sat, like a perfect little angel pig. There was a murmur of excitement as a bunch of people scooted their chairs closer. Chip let out a nervous snort, stood up, and squirmed.

Milla asked everyone to stay as quiet and still as possible. Once Chip had calmed down again, she began her presentation. "My family adopted Chip six months ago. We took him in after his original family realized they weren't able to care for him. Chip was advertised as a teacup pig. The person who sold him promised that he wouldn't get any bigger than twenty pounds, about the size of a small dog." Milla took a deep breath. "But the truth is, the only way to keep a pig that small is to starve it. That kind of treatment is not fair to an animal. It's not healthy or kind."

Milla glanced at her classmates, who all seemed really interested in what she was saying. Even better, her mom was nodding her approval at the back of the room. So far, so good!

"Chip's original family was lucky we were able to take him in," she went on. "Many people who get pigs as pets learn too late that they're not easy *or* small animals. There are many, many pigs who end up in pig rescue centers—or worse—because their owners don't know what they're getting themselves into." Milla patted her beloved pet, then handed him a piece of apple from the bag in her pocket. She was happy he was behaving so well.

"The lesson I learned when we adopted Chip is, it's very important to do a *lot* of research on an animal's care and training needs before you bring it home. People often get pets because they seem fun—and by the time they learn how much work they can be, it's usually too late to change your mind. Then you end up with an unhappy pet *and* an unhappy family."

When Milla finished, she felt very proud. A bunch of hands went up, and she tried to answer as many questions as she could. Her classmates wanted to know what kind of tricks Chip could do, what his favorite foods and toys were, and where he slept at night. Milla could tell everyone was very curious and excited, but she could also tell that Chip was growing restless. She knew she should get him out of school before he got too crabby. That was when Milla reached into her pocket and discovered she had run out of treats. She knew it was definitely time to wrap things up and get her pig out of there!

At that exact moment, the leg of someone's chair scraped across the floor. It made a loud screech, and Chip let out a startled squeal. Then, with a powerful tug, he pulled his leash out of Milla's hand. Her pig raced out of the classroom, away from the spooky sound, his little feet clattering on the hard linoleum floor.

Milla chased him, but Chip was surprisingly quick! He ran down the fifth-grade hall, nearly knocking Ms. Burniac off her feet. He slid around the corner and dashed past the lunchroom. Milla ran behind, trying to grab his leash. She had to figure out some way to get him to stop running!

Thinking fast, she ducked inside the lunchroom;

there was a chance school breakfast would still be out. As luck would have it, there was a carton of bananas right by the lunchroom door. Milla grabbed two, then hustled back into the hall.

She turned another corner just in time to see Chip knock over a chair in the second-grade hall. He crashed into a wall, pulling down a mural the first graders had made. The speedy pig zoomed down the kindergarten hallway. Milla peeled open a banana as she ran and shouted, "Chip! Do you want a treat? Banana, buddy!"

Chip squealed to a stop outside one of the kindergarten classrooms. He spun around at the exact moment Piper's little sister, Finley, poked her head into the hall. The little girl looked at the pig, then up at Milla, and bleated, "Baaaa." Chip snorted in response; then he trotted over to Milla and waited patiently for his banana.

"Baaaa," Finley said again. She waved at Milla and Chip and returned to her classroom. It was almost as if a pig on the loose was part of

Finley's *usual* day in kindergarten.

With a relieved laugh, Milla grabbed Chip's leash off the floor. She guided her pet toward the school's front doors. As she made her way down the hall, she saw her mom and a furious-looking Ms. Burniac. The unimpressed looks on both of their faces told Milla everything she needed to know: the plan to prove herself responsible had backfired . . . big-time. That day's adventure had *not* gone according to plan!

7
PLAN B

Even though Milla's first *big* plan to prove she was responsible had not gone exactly as she'd hoped, she wasn't going to give up. She had to get that permission slip signed, no matter what! So it was time to move on to plan B—and fast.

The trouble was, Milla wasn't sure what plan B *was* yet. She had spent the weekend and the first part of the school week doing plenty of little things to try to prove she was independent, trustworthy, and responsible. But so far nothing seemed like it had been big enough to show her moms she was ready for an overnight adventure in the great wide somewhere *without* them watching out for her.

So Milla brought her Daring Dreamers journal out to the playground at recess on Thursday, hoping some fresh air might help her come up with a few outstanding ideas. She sat on a swing, holding her journal open in her lap, and waited for inspiration to strike. While she waited, she jotted down some of the other ideas her club-mates had suggested at their last meeting:

* Cook dinner for the family?

* Pack my own lunches all week —DONE!

* Clean my room —DONE! (But no one can tell, since books are piled everywhere!)

* Clear the table after dinner —already do this!

* Pet-sitting —doesn't taking care of Chip every day count?!?!

Piper plunked down on the swing next to Milla, tipping her head upside down as she pumped her legs. "Adventure Camp permission slips are due Monday," she reminded Milla. "So what's your next plan, Stan?"

"Dunno." Milla chewed the cap of her pen thoughtfully. "I'm going to write until I figure it out."

"Hey, Milla!" Zahra ran toward the swings, smiling broadly. "I was looking all over for you at recess yesterday. I heard what happened with your pig visit. Sounds like things got a little crazy, huh?"

Milla sighed and rolled her eyes. "Yeah. Let's just say Chip's first day of school didn't exactly go the way I'd planned."

"I've been thinking about your permission slip problem and I had another idea," Zahra said. "Where do you live . . . and do you ever walk to school?"

"No, I always get a ride," Milla said, unsure where Zahra was going with her question. "I live on Fifteenth and Dupont."

"Would you be interested in walking to school together sometime?" Zahra asked. "I thought maybe that would help you prove your independence. A short walk to school isn't a huge deal, right? But it might help your moms get used to the idea of you going places without them."

Milla considered the suggestion. "It's not a bad idea," she said. "In fact, it could work!"

Piper sat upright on her swing, her cheeks flushed. "I wish I lived near you guys. I'd love to walk to school with you." She frowned. "But then you'd have to walk with Finley, and we'd all have to talk in animal voices." She scuffed her shoes in the dirt under her swing. "Finley *still* thinks she's a sheep, and her teacher has had to call my parents to talk about it every night this week." She kicked off the ground and swung high in the air. "So yeah, never mind. I'll just walk my little lamb to school every day instead."

"Do your parents let you walk to school?" Milla asked Zahra. She wasn't sure *hers* would be okay with the idea, but if she told her moms Zahra had permission, it might make them more willing to consider the idea.

"My parents are pretty strict about a lot of stuff," Zahra said. "But they promised they would let me walk to school this year if I have someone to walk with. My mom will definitely want to call yours to talk through all the details, since she likes to know who I'm hanging out with. Would that be okay?"

"Of course," Milla said. "It might help to have my mom talk to yours, actually."

Since Zahra's family only lived a few blocks from Milla's, they exchanged phone numbers and made a plan of where to meet up the next morning. They decided they could connect at the corner of Fourteenth Street and Elmwood at eight-thirty and walk the two-thirds of a mile down the hill to school. When Milla told Ruby about their walking plan during class that afternoon, Ruby asked if she could join them, too. Milla was super excited and couldn't wait to see what her parents would say.

It took a lot of pleading and a long call to talk through all the details with Zahra's mom later that night—but Milla's parents actually agreed to the plan! So the next morning, Milla got up and dressed extra early, took care of all her Chip chores, and made sure her homework was done and in her backpack long before she needed to head out the door.

"Are you sure about this?" Milla's mum asked, glancing out the window. She had just gotten home from an overnight shift at the hospital and was still in her scrubs. With a yawn, she said, "I hardly ever get to drive you to school, and it looks a little like it might rain. Why don't I just drive all three of you?"

Milla gave her mum a look. "It's sunny. And we *want* to walk."

"There are clouds," her mum said, stifling another yawn.

"Mum . . ."

"I know, I know." Her mum held up her hands in surrender. "It's just hard for me, seeing you growing up like this. I've never met any of these girls, and you don't know what could happen on the walk to school. What if you get lost?"

Milla groaned. "It's a straight shot to school. It would take serious effort for us to get lost. We'd have to blindfold ourselves and spin around in circles and—"

Her mum laughed and cut her off. "Yeah, yeah, I get it. I'm being overly concerned."

Milla said, "Would it make you less worried if you drove to school and waited there to be sure we make it safely?"

With a slight shrug, her mum muttered, "Yeah, probably."

Milla laughed. "Okay, then, why don't you do that?" Milla was willing to do whatever it took to get her mum to trust her. As she gathered her things and made her way toward the door, she said, "And, Mum? You, me, and Mom really need to talk about the fifth-grade overnight. Permission slips are due first thing next week, and—"

"Yeah, I know—your mom told me about it. We will," her mum said. Milla grabbed her lunch bag. "But now is definitely not the time. Your mom already left for work, and you have to get moving or your friends will leave without you."

"Mum, I have ten minutes to make it to our meeting spot . . . which is less than two blocks away."

"Be safe," her mum called after her. "Be responsible. Be careful."

"I always am," Milla promised. She gave Chip a hug, tucked him under his favorite blanket, then skipped down the street and around the corner. While she waited for her friends, Milla tilted her head up and let the sun warm her face. She was excited to spend some time with Zahra and Ruby so she could get to know both of them a little better. If today's walk worked out, maybe they could make walking to school together part of their regular routine!

"Hi, Milla!" Ruby called, hustling across the street to their meeting spot.

Zahra appeared from the other direction a few moments later, and the three girls set off down the hill toward school. While they walked, they talked about their teachers, Zahra's art, and their families. Milla told the other girls that her mum was originally from England, and her parents met when they were backpacking through Europe after college. It turned out Zahra's parents had also immigrated to America—from Somalia, in Africa—when they were young, before Zahra and her little brother were born. Ruby's parents were recently divorced, so she and her twin brother split time between two houses.

"Isn't it strange that the three of us might have never gotten to know each other if it weren't for the Daring Dreamers Club?" Ruby asked.

"I'm glad we were put in a group together,"

Zahra said. "What do you think of the advisory program so far?"

"Ms. Bancroft is great," Milla said.

"I wasn't sure what to expect when Ms. Burniac first told us we were getting advisors this year," Ruby told them. "My mom is a *financial* advisor, so I got this picture in my head of meetings where we would all sit around talking about money." She grinned, then added, "Either that, or Ms. Bancroft would yell at us to clean our desks or do our homework like my mom is always doing."

Milla laughed. "I can't imagine Ms. Bancroft yelling at anyone. Especially not about homework." She paused, before saying something aloud that had been on her mind for a while. "What do you guys think Ms. Bancroft did before she came to Walter Roy? She talked about how she dreamed of one day living in the woods, like Sleeping Beauty or Snow White. But a music classroom isn't exactly the great outdoors."

"We could ask her," Ruby said.

"I feel like she'll tell us sometime," Zahra said. "When it makes sense."

Milla nodded. "I bet you're right." She longed to know more about Ms. Bancroft—how had Aurora and Snow White helped her figure out her big dream? And how had that dream led her to a job as their music teacher? Though she would love to come right out and ask, Milla knew how much some people valued their privacy. So she decided she would wait for Ms. Bancroft to tell them her story when she was good and ready. In the meantime, Milla had started to write several different made-up stories about the kind of girl she imagined Ms. Bancroft had been as a kid.

"We should walk to school together every day," Ruby said. "This totally beats the bus!"

Suddenly, Milla stopped and pointed. A half-block ahead of them, a small, fluffy white dog stood alone on the sidewalk. It had a collar but no leash. "Do you think that little dog is supposed to be out on its own?" she asked.

Ruby began to race across the street toward the pup, but Milla held out a hand to stop her. "It's never a good idea to approach an unfamiliar dog," she warned. "Besides, we don't want to scare it and make it run even farther from home. Some dogs get nervous when they're chased."

Milla and her friends crossed the street slowly. "Hey, I know this dog!" Milla told Zahra and Ruby when they got a little closer to the pup. "It's Xena, one of my mom's patients at the clinic. She's super friendly, and I'm pretty sure her owner lives near here. I've seen the two of them walking past our house." Milla crouched down and whistled for Xena to come. Xena crept forward, wagging her tail. But when she was just a few feet away, the little pup turned and ran off in the other direction, her floppy ears bouncing with each step.

"What do we do now?" Ruby asked desperately. "If we don't keep moving, we're going to be late for school. But I don't want to ditch Xena!"

Milla was relieved she wasn't the only one who'd been thinking that.

"Maybe she'll let us get close enough to read her tags?" Milla said. "I bet there's a phone number on her collar." Even as she said it, Milla thought about how furious her parents would be if she was late for school. But on the other hand, she'd been taught to help a creature in need whenever possible. So without giving it another moment's consideration, Milla and her friends set off across the street, slowly trailing after Xena and calling for her to come.

As they made their way down the next block, heading away from school, Xena stayed about twenty feet ahead of them. But every once in a while, she would glance back over her shoulder to check that the girls were still there. Milla knew this little game could go on forever.

Suddenly, she had an idea. She reached into her hoodie pocket and pulled one of Chip's treats out of a plastic bag. She usually kept a few snacks on hand, just in case. "Do you want a treat?" Milla called, softly but firmly. It had worked with Chip when he was on the run at school—maybe the trick would work with Xena, too!

The word "treat" quickly got Xena's attention.

The little pup turned and trotted straight toward them. She reached out to take the snack from Milla's open palm. As soon as Xena was close enough, Milla took hold of the dog's collar.

"There's a phone number!" Zahra said happily.

Ruby pulled out her cell phone and dialed the number on Xena's tag. Someone answered right away, and Ruby explained the situation and their location. When she hung up, she told the other girls, "Xena's owner has been out searching the neighborhood all morning! She's in her car just a couple blocks away, and said she'll be here in two minutes."

When the pup's owner pulled up, she jumped out of her car and ran across the street, saying, "Thank you, thank you, thank you," over and over again. "I'm *so* happy you found her. I accidentally left the back gate unlatched and she must have dashed out. She never leaves the yard! Thank you, thank you, thank you."

"No problem," Milla said, passing the shivering dog into its relieved owner's arms. "Have a good day!"

As soon as Xena and her owner drove off, the girls gave each other high-fives. But there wasn't much time to celebrate—school would be starting in less than five minutes. So the three girls grabbed their backpacks and raced the rest of the way down the hill, trying to beat the bell. As they rounded the corner onto the school lot, Milla spotted her mum pacing next to her car. They had arrived much later then Milla said they would, and she had a feeling her mum was both angry and worried.

Milla tossed her mum a quick wave. Eleanor glanced down at her watch, and yelled, "What took you so long? You're going to be late for school."

Just as Milla began to explain, the bell rang. Milla called out, "I'll tell you everything later!" Then she blew her mum a kiss and raced after her friends toward the main doors.

Deep down, Milla was sure she'd done the right thing when she stopped to help Xena find her way home. Even if it meant getting in trouble, she would never abandon a creature in need. She only hoped her parents would agree that she'd made the right decision. But Milla had a sinking suspicion that the choice to help Xena might have just cost her the overnight trip.

Zahra

Me:

* Artistic ~~and~~ colorful
* Hardworking
* Unique
* Private
* Spiritual
* Independent
* Kind
* Quirky (Is that the same as unique? I guess the point is, I don't always feel like I fit in.)

Princesses:

~~Snow White~~
~~Sleeping Beauty (Aurora)~~
~~Pocahontas~~
~~Ariel~~
~~Jasmine~~
~~Tiana~~

~~Merida~~
~~Belle~~
~~Mulan~~
~~Rapunzel~~
Cinderella

One thing you should know about me is that I value my uniqueness and I've never really liked comparing myself to others. But the princess I probably feel the closest connection to is Cinderella. Does that surprise you? Here's why: Much like me, Cinderella is really good at taking ordinary, left-behind scraps of clothing and leftover items and turning them into something beautiful. Also like me, she is kind, hardworking, refuses to let anyone get her down, and doesn't always fit in (her reasons for that are very different from mine, of course—but you get the general idea).

After you gave us this princess assignment, I started to wonder something: Do you think of yourself as our fairy godmother, Ms. Bancroft? In some ways, it seems like that's the role you're playing with the Daring Dreamers Club. You want us to tell you our dreams and make wishes so that you can help grant them. Even though I like the idea of having a fairy godmother, I've always been pretty good at making my own dreams come true. So I already know that, like Cinderella, I can achieve my dreams on my own—but a little extra help never hurts.

Because you are sort of like the group's fairy godmother, I think I might make you a magic wand. Although, if you ask me, hard work is the most powerful magic. I still think you need a wand. I know you don't grant wishes in the usual fairy godmother way, but no matter what, a wand will give you some extra sparkle when you're directing the fifth-grade choir. Everyone likes a little sparkle, right? (Also, you seem like the kind of person who could have a lot of fun with a wand.)

8
PiG PARTY

"Less than a week until we set off on our adventure to the great wide somewhere," Ms. Bancroft said on Friday, at the next official meeting of the Daring Dreamers Club. She and Milla exchanged a smile—Milla had, of course, recognized the line Ms. B had borrowed from one of Belle's songs. "Have you all turned in your signed permission slips?"

Ruby, Zahra, Piper, and Mariana all nodded. But Milla shook her head. "Not yet. My parents and I *still* haven't had a chance to sit down and talk about it as a family—and none of my plans have worked out the way they were supposed to. So as much as I want adventure in the great wide somewhere, it looks like I'm going to be stuck here in this small, provincial life a little longer."

"Aw, man," Ruby said with a frown.

Zahra reached over and patted Milla on the shoulder. "Sorry, Milla."

"That stinks," Mari added.

"Can you fill us in?" Ms. Bancroft asked.

"Well, I'm pretty sure everyone at school heard about how my pet pig ruined plan A," Milla said. Ruby laughed. Since she was the only other person in their group who had Mr. Poloski for homeroom, she was the only member of the Daring Dreamers Club who had witnessed Chocolate Chip's escape firsthand. Whenever someone talked about the events of that day, Ruby cracked up all over again.

"I did hear about your pig's visit to school," Ms. Bancroft said, trying to keep herself from laughing. "But it sounds like you acted very responsibly and handled the situation the best you could. I heard you got everything quickly under control."

"Things should never have gotten *out* of control in the first place," Milla said. She then told Ms. Bancroft about the lost dog she, Zahra, and Ruby had found on their walk to school that morning. They had already told Piper and Mari what had happened during recess. When Milla finished the story, she said, "So Xena the lost dog sort of put a kink in plan B. I *promised* my mum I would walk straight to school. There's no way they're going to trust me after this. They'll never let me go anywhere without an adult again."

Mari said quietly, "But when they hear the story, won't your moms be happy you helped the dog? I'm sure when you explain why you were late, they'll understand."

Ms. Bancroft nodded. "Mari makes a good point. You had to make a choice in each of those moments . . . with your pig during his school visit, and with the lost dog this morning. Both times, you acted in the way you thought was right. That's part of growing up and gaining independence, Milla. Sometimes things don't go exactly as planned, and you have to make quick decisions in less-than-perfect situations."

Milla nodded. "Yeah, I guess that's true." She hoped her moms would see it that way, too.

"Think about the choice Belle was forced to make in *Beauty and the Beast*," Ms. Bancroft said. "She had to choose between saving her father and giving up her own freedom to explore the world. She made the choice that felt right. She sacrificed her own dream to help another."

Milla didn't say it aloud, but she really hoped that by helping a lost dog she hadn't sacrificed her own chance at adventure on the fifth-grade overnight!

All of a sudden, Piper started laughing.

"What's so funny?" Zahra asked.

"My sister stopped talking in sheep language

long enough to tell me about the end of Milla's pig chase," Piper said, laughing harder. "I really wish I had been there to see it."

"It was a disaster," Milla said, laughing. "I don't think the little stinker's going to be invited back anytime soon."

"Bummer," Mari said. "I really wanted to meet him."

"Do you want to come over this weekend and hang out with him?" Milla offered. "Chip *loves* visitors. You could all come."

"All of us?" Zahra asked, looking a little uncomfortable.

Milla nodded. "Yeah. It would be like an extra meeting of the Daring Dreamers Club." She turned to Ms. Bancroft. "Are we *allowed* to meet without you, Ms. B?"

"Of course," Ms. Bancroft said, smiling. "In fact, I'd encourage it."

"I'm definitely in," Mari said.

"Me too," Ruby agreed.

"Me three!" Piper said.

"I have to be honest about something. . . ." Zahra took a deep breath and said, "In Islamic faith, pigs are considered impure. As a Muslim, I don't eat pork and I really don't like the idea of playing with Chip, either. I love animals, but even the thought of touching a pig makes me uncomfortable."

"Oh!" Milla said. This surprised her. She knew Zahra was a Muslim, because of her headscarf, but she didn't know much about what that meant. Piper didn't eat pork, either, because she was Jewish. And ever since they'd adopted Chip, Milla had refused to eat pork, too—for obvious reasons. But that was a matter of choice, not faith or religion.

Milla was very happy Zahra felt comfortable being honest with her. "If you can't come over," Milla told her, "I definitely understand. I'll figure out another time for Mari to hang out with Chip. But I don't want to have a club meeting if you can't be there—that wouldn't be fair."

"Thanks, Milla," Zahra said with a grateful smile. After a beat, she went on, "I think it would be okay if I came over to your house as long as I keep my distance. Of course, I need to check with my parents to see what they think. But because it's for a school group, I have a feeling they'll probably say it's fine."

"Call me tonight and let me know," Milla told her. She knew her moms would love to meet her new friends and hoped everything would work out. "I promise to keep Chip far away from you, Zahra." She turned to Mari and Ruby and said, "And just a heads-up, if you guys *are* planning to play with Chip . . . don't wear anything you don't want to get dirty, okay? Prince Chip is famous for his slobbery kisses."

★★★

"I brought snacks!" Piper announced when she arrived at Milla's house the next day. Zahra had called Milla after school on Friday and told her she would be able to come over—which meant their meeting was on! Milla had been waiting impatiently all morning for her friends to arrive. Piper showed up first. "It's an invention I'm calling Dream Big bars. Nut-free *and* pig-safe. Things got a little wonky with the batter, so they don't look all that pretty, but they taste okay."

"I'm sure they're great," Milla said. "And Chocolate Chip will be very happy you thought of him."

Ruby showed up next, with her twin brother in tow. "Can I meet your pig, too?" Henry asked.

"Sure, come on. He's in the backyard," Milla said, holding the door open for both of them. Even though Henry was wild and crazy at school, Milla thought he seemed like a really nice guy. He always included everyone when he organized recess games, and Milla had a feeling there was more to Henry than the loud, show-offy kid who was often getting into trouble for goofing off. Henry kneeled right down on the ground with Chip to play and cuddle. He was like a whole different person outside of school!

Henry had only been there for a few minutes when Ruby yanked him up and announced, "Time's up, Hen. You're not a member of the Daring Dreamers Club, so it's time for you to go."

Henry grumbled and said, "Your advisory group is way more fun than mine is. You have a pig mascot!"

"Lucky for us, sad for you," Ruby said, shrugging. She led Henry to the front door and added, "Maybe you should do something to make your group more interesting. Our club rocks because we made it that way."

When Mari arrived, she seemed a little unsure of how to act around Chip. "I've never met a pig in person before," she said. "Do you pet him like a dog?" Milla let Mariana feed him some snacks to help break the ice, and soon the little pig curled up and fell asleep with his head on Mari's lap.

"I think he likes you," Milla told her.

"I know *I* like him!" Mari said.

Zahra was the last to arrive, and she came bearing gifts! She had made glass mosaic picture frames for everyone in the group. "These are beautiful!" Milla said, giving her a hug. "Thanks so much, Zahra."

"No problem," Zahra said. "I like to make stuff for friends."

Milla said, "I'll get my mom to take a Daring Dreamers Club photo, and then we can all frame them to take home!"

After they ate Piper's bars, the girls headed out to the backyard. "One of my favorite things," Milla told her friends, "is setting up adventures for Chocolate Chip here in the backyard. I make little stage sets using plants and old dolls or empty cardboard boxes and toy cars or whatever. Then I pretend Chip is the main character in a story and

I write about the things he does."

"Can we do that?" Ruby asked. "We could build a world together."

"For sure!" Milla said.

As Ruby and Piper worked together to build roads and tunnels, Mari and Milla cut and colored cardboard buildings that Chip could destroy. Meanwhile, Zahra made tons of tiny stars and tied them to low-hanging tree branches at the back of the yard—keeping a nice, comfortable distance between herself and Chip.

When Piper grew bored with making roads, she decided their land would be much more interesting if she whipped up a batch of lava and turned an old plastic pot into a volcano. Zahra and Milla helped her gather ingredients for her concoction from the kitchen, and then Piper mixed it all up in the middle of the yard.

While the girls created their land, Chip was his usual charming self. He snorted and raced around the yard, knocking things over almost as soon as they were constructed. No one seemed to mind, since he was having so much fun and being very entertaining. At one point, Chip got stuck inside a cardboard box and he rolled around and around on the ground, trying to escape. By the time Milla had freed him, everyone was laughing like crazy.

As she worked on reassembling a three-box-tall cardboard skyscraper, Ruby asked, "So when are you going to talk to your parents about the permission slip, Milla? They have to be turned in on Monday—we leave for camp next Thursday!"

"Believe me, I know." Milla said, poking a stick into the pot of lava. "My mum is off tonight and my mom isn't on call at the clinic, so all three of us are finally going to be home at the same time."

"Have you thought about what you're going to say?" Zahra asked.

"Yeah, I think so," Milla said. "And I offered to cook dinner tonight, too. One last chance to prove that I'm responsible."

Piper clapped. "What are you going to cook?"

"I haven't figured that part out yet," Milla muttered.

Suddenly, Mariana's watch dinged. She glanced down and said, "Yikes. My mom is supposed to pick me up in five minutes! We have a swim team potluck tonight."

"What time is it?" Ruby asked.

"Four-thirty," Mari said.

Ruby groaned. "Ugh. For the first time in my whole life, I actually wish I didn't have soccer practice today. I have to go."

"I'm sorry, Milla, but I should probably leave, too," Zahra said. "We cook family dinner every Saturday night, and I promised my mom I'd be home in time to help."

"Maybe we could do this again?" Mari suggested quietly. "What do you guys think about having an extra club meeting outside of our regular meeting days once a week? This was fun."

"I love that idea!" Piper said and everyone else agreed. The girls decided they could trade off going to different people's houses each week, or use recess and lunch for extra meeting time.

After the others had left, Milla and Piper spent a few minutes cleaning up the backyard while Chip cleaned up the crumbled remnants of Piper's Dream Big bars. "Want some help cooking dinner?" Piper asked.

"I'd love that," Milla said. "I was thinking about making pancakes and eggs."

Piper wrinkled her nose. "No. You can do better than that. What do your parents like to eat?"

"I know my mom loves popovers, and my mum loves pasta," Milla said, shrugging. "But I don't know how to make either of those things."

"Not to worry. As long as you have some basic supplies in the fridge, we can make this a dinner to remember," Piper promised. "Come on."

Nearly an hour later, the kitchen looked a lot like the backyard did after Chocolate Chip had been extra destructive. There was flour everywhere, slimy bits of broken eggshell were stuck to the bottom of the sink, and every single bowl the Bannister-Cooks owned was dirty. Milla had tried to clean up while Piper cooked, but her friend was surprisingly quick and messy—kind of like Chip!

"I know it *looks* bad in here," Piper said, surveying the mess. She pushed her glasses up on the bridge of her nose. "But dinner is going to *taste* really good. I'll help clean up, too. Promise."

Milla laughed. "I'm sure it will be yummy and my parents will be very impressed with my much-improved cooking skills." She had just begun to fill the sink with soapy water to wash a batch of dishes when she heard the phone ring in the other room.

A second later, Milla's mom poked her head around the corner. "Piper, your dad is coming to get you." Her eyes bugged out of her head when she saw the state of the kitchen. "Whoa . . . what kind of natural disaster struck in here?"

Milla stepped forward and tried to block her mom's view of the mess. "Nothing to see here!"

"He's coming now?" Piper asked.

"Afraid so," Milla's mom said. "He's swinging by to pick you up in two minutes. Grab your stuff and wait out front."

Piper mouthed, "I'm sorry," then headed for the front door.

As soon as Piper was gone, Milla's mom shook her head and surveyed the situation in the kitchen. "I'm really sorry about the mess, Mom," Milla said calmly. "But Piper helped me make a delicious dinner—popovers and homemade pasta, both gluten-free! And the best part is, you don't have to do anything. I'm on it."

"It's been a really long week." Her mom took a deep breath. Milla could tell she was trying hard not to get angry. "To be totally honest, this is not what I wanted to deal with tonight."

"I'll clean everything up," Milla promised. Still her mom refused to leave the kitchen. Milla tried again. "You don't have to do anything, Mom. This is all my responsibility. Trust me."

But it was no use arguing. With another big sigh, her mom grabbed a dishcloth and began wiping the mess on the counter. It seemed that yet another one of Milla's plans had gone all wrong.

9
DINNER DISASTER

Milla was frustrated. Over and over again, she had tried to prove that she was capable and self-sufficient. But not one of her attempts had worked out quite the way she had planned.

Instead of demonstrating that she was a responsible pet owner, her pig got loose at school.

Instead of showing her parents that she was independent enough to walk to school with friends, Milla had been late to class and lost their trust.

Instead of presenting her parents with a beautiful home-cooked dinner, she had delivered her mom a mess.

While she worked with her mom to clean up the kitchen, Milla thought about what she might say to her parents when they all sat down to eat. Would she be able to convince them that she should go on the trip with the rest of her class-mates? She knew she had to focus on how she had always wanted to be a great adventurer, to set out and see the world. Just like Belle. And make sure they understood this was her first big chance to have a grand adventure on her own.

But after the way her week had gone, Milla was starting to wonder if she really *was* ready to take care of herself out in the great wide some-where. Maybe there was a reason her parents kept her close and protected. Maybe she should just stick to reading and writing stories about other peoples' adventures—it was a whole lot easier to write your way out of problems than it was to fix things in *real* life.

Milla fed Chip his dinner and then set the table. Thanks to her mom's help, the kitchen was clean by the time dinner was ready. She put on some classical music and lit a few candles. They didn't get to have family dinners very often, and Milla wanted it to feel special.

"This looks delicious," her mum said. "Thanks for cooking, love. I'm very impressed. This looks like a restaurant meal."

"You're welcome," Milla told her with a small smile. She looked at her mom and said, again, "I'm sorry about the mess."

"I'm sorry I snapped at you about it," her mom said, settling in at the table. She grabbed a warm popover and pulled it open. A puff of steam escaped from inside the hot roll. "I've had a couple of hard days this week. But I shouldn't have taken it out on you."

"I really was going to clean up," Milla said slowly. Her plate was still empty. Suddenly, she didn't feel much like eating. "You didn't need to pick up after me. I could have done it myself."

"I know I didn't *need* to," her mom said,

frowning. "But you cooked dinner—the least I could do is help clean up."

"Oh," Milla said, confused. "I thought . . . I thought you cleaned up after me because you didn't think I would do a good job on my own."

"That's a silly thing to assume," her mom said. "I'm sure you'd do a fine job, but who likes to clean alone? It's always nice to have some help."

Milla nodded. All of a sudden she felt like she was going to cry. She swallowed, trying to push the tears back down—but it was too late. There was a long silence, and then Milla's mum said, "Hon, is everything okay? Did things not go well with your friends this afternoon?"

"No, it's not that," Milla mumbled. "We had a lot of fun."

"Then what's eating you?" her mom asked. "You're obviously down about something."

"It's the fifth-grade overnight," Milla blurted out. Her words came spilling out in a big rush. "I really want to go to Adventure Camp with my class. So badly! I know you don't think I'm ready to take care of myself, but I want you to realize that I'm not a little kid anymore. It's just one night!"

Her parents stared at her without saying anything.

"All week, I've been trying to prove to you that I'm responsible and independent. But nothing has worked out the way I wanted it to!" Milla heaved a sigh. "And now I don't even know if I *should* be allowed to go. Maybe I don't—"

Milla's mom held her fork up and cut her off. "Whoa, whoa, whoa. Milla, why have you been trying to prove you're responsible and independent?"

"Because I need my permission slip signed," Milla said impatiently. "And I know you don't want me to go, so I was trying to change your minds."

"Who said we don't want you to go?" Milla's mum asked, furrowing her brow.

"Every time I've tried to talk to you about it, you've told me it's not a good time," Milla said. "And I know you worry about my allergies, and about me getting hurt again—but everyone else in fifth grade is going. I know I've never spent a night away from you guys before, but I think it's about time. I'm never going to be a great explorer if I have to stay inside this house forever!"

"Hold on. I thought permission slips aren't due until Monday," her mom said, confused.

"Yeah," Milla answered quietly.

"So let's talk about it now," her mum said. "First off, what's this about you trying to prove you're responsible? We *know* you're responsible, love."

"You do?"

Milla's mom nodded her agreement. "For one thing, you take great care of Chocolate Chip."

"But I let him get loose at school," Milla said, wishing she didn't have to remind them.

"Yeah," her mom said, laughing. "Because he's a sneaky, strong little guy. But thanks to your quick thinking, you got things under control in no time."

"And I know I screwed up yesterday when I walked to school with my friends," Milla said. "I promised Mum she could trust me to go straight there, but I didn't want to leave Xena out on the street all by herself—"

Milla's mum cut her off. "Naturally, I was worried when you got to school much later than I'd expected you. A million worst-case scenarios went through my mind—it's my nature. But you obviously did what you had to do, and you made a smart decision in the moment. It all worked out."

"And I made a huge mess of dinner tonight." Milla sighed and picked a chunk off one of the popovers. "I just wanted everything to go perfectly."

Her mom tipped her chin up and told her, "Even if none of your plans have gone exactly the way they were supposed to, nothing terrible has happened. You see that, right?"

"Great adventures rarely go as planned, love," her mum said. "Your mom and I know that better than anyone."

Milla's parents both started laughing. "Remember the time our boots were stolen at the market outside Florence?" her mom asked. She turned to Milla and explained, "We'd taken them off to give our feet a rest after a long hike, and someone took them while we were buying oranges! We had to go barefoot for a whole day."

"Then there was the night our train in Paris got in so late that they gave away our beds at the hostel," her mum said, grinning. "We spent the night wandering around the city, trying to stay awake."

"You can't plan for every problem that might arise in life," Milla's mom said. "The most important thing is that you know how to troubleshoot. Lucky for you, you're persistent, smart, and very independent, Milla."

"And you know how to think on your feet," her mum added. "We worry about you and try to support you through everything because that's a parent's job. But we've never once doubted how responsible you are."

"Really?" Milla asked, smiling.

"We never meant for you to think you

wouldn't be allowed to go on the overnight," her mom said. "When I told you I wanted to wait to talk about it as a family, that's what I meant. I wanted to talk it over to be sure *you* feel comfortable being there without us."

"But if you want to go, of course you can go!" her mum finished.

"*Really* really?" Milla squeaked.

"Really really," her mom said. "Bring me that permission slip so I can sign it right now. Your fifth-grade adventure awaits."

Milla

Once upon a time, there was a girl who finally had a signed permission slip!

That girl? It's <u>me</u>. I'm going to Adventure Camp with all the other fifth graders! And you know what? I'm feeling like Belle when I say: for once it feels quite grand, to have my parents understand . . . that I want more than this provincial life!

When I finally got a chance to talk with my parents about the overnight, we had a great conversation. We talked all about the field trip, and my dreams of adventure, and they both said a lot of really nice things about me. They said that I'm responsible, and they trust me, and I know how to think on my feet. I guess, deep down, those are things I already knew about myself, but it felt good to hear them say it out loud.

Here's why: Since my moms have always been there to pick up the pieces when things go wrong, I guess maybe I've always worried (a little bit) that I wouldn't know what to do if something bad happened when they weren't around. But now that I know my moms trust me, I feel a lot surer about myself. Maybe I didn't need to prove to my _parents_ that I'm responsible and can take care of myself. Maybe the person who really needed that proof was _me_!

Ever since we got the Disney Princess assignment for the Daring Dreamers Club, I've been thinking about Belle (and what kind of person she is) a lot. Originally I thought she and I were only alike because of our dreams of adventure and because we both like to read. But after talking to the other girls in the club, here's what I've come to realize: Like Belle, who could see the Beast's warm heart hiding behind his rough exterior, I always try to see the best in everyone. But I've also realized that it can sometimes be hard to see the best parts of yourself, unless someone else points them out. You know?

Now more than ever, it's extra important to me that the overnight go well. Luckily, I've read enough nonfiction adventure books that I should be able to troubleshoot almost any situation! But I sure hope I'm right. Because this is my first real chance to prove to my parents (and ME!) that I can survive an adventure of my own without someone watching out for me.

10
CAMP SWITCHEROO

"Load up, campers!" Ms. Bancroft stood outside the door of one of the two camp buses and waved a clipboard in the air. "All aboard. We've got a big day ahead of us!"

It was total chaos outside Walter Roy Elementary, even though school wouldn't officially start for nearly an hour. The bus ride to Adventure Camp was three hours long, so the fifth graders had arrived early to get on the road. They were supposed to get to camp before lunch so they could spend the whole afternoon exploring.

Milla and the rest of the Daring Dreamers

Club had been assigned seats next to each other for the bus ride. All five girls had brought along games and activities to share, and Ruby had put a little music player into her bag. No one dared turn the sound up very loud, but they had a lot of fun leaning in close to the music, and then singing along at the top of their lungs. They got the rest of the bus to sing, too, before they had even left the school parking lot.

"Wow, Mari, you can *sing*!" Ruby declared as the bus zoomed north on the highway.

Mariana smiled shyly. "I usually only sing in the shower, and when I visit my *abuela*. My voice is terrible next to hers—my *abuela* is a beautiful singer."

"Are you crazy?" Ruby said, bouncing up and down. "You can't hide a voice like that! You should try out for the fifth-grade musical. You're looking forward to the Adventure Camp skits too, right? If you can act *and* sing, you'll be a shoo-in."

Milla agreed. "You really should try out, Mariana. You have a beautiful voice."

"I don't know . . . ," Mari said, but Milla could tell she was flattered by the compliments. "Maybe."

The conversation ended when Henry Fawcett waved to get his sister's attention from his seat near the front of the bus. Ruby didn't notice him at first, so Henry threw a balled-up piece of paper at her head and yelled, "Yo, little sis!"

Ruby narrowed her eyes at him under her baseball cap. "We're *twins*. Don't 'little sis' me, Hen."

"Who's older?" Henry said, shrugging. For the first time ever, Milla realized how much Henry and Ruby looked alike—especially today, when they were wearing matching caps and soccer jackets. With her ponytail tucked up inside her hat, Ruby could easily have been mistaken for her brother. "Me, by six minutes. Fact. Older *and* wiser," he bragged.

Ruby laughed. "As if. I'm so clearly the smart twin."

"Aw, Ruby. Honesty is the best policy," Henry said. "But if you want to *prove* you're wiser, how about you trade seats with Levi and help me win trivia?"

"You're playing trivia?" Ruby asked, scrambling to her feet. She stepped into the aisle. "Without me?"

A second later, one of the chaperones at the back of the bus yelled, "Stay in your seat, please!"

"Can my brother and I swap spots?" Ruby asked, plunking down in her seat. She looked back at Ms. Bancroft, who was sitting a few rows behind them and across the aisle. "Just for a little bit?"

"Sorry," Ms. Bancroft said apologetically. "No switching seats."

"Please?" Ruby begged. She half stood up again, as though she was expecting Ms. Bancroft to take her side.

"Don't make me use my wand," Ms. Bancroft replied, trying to look stern. She held up the magic wand Zahra had given her that morning before they left. She pointed it at Ruby, twirled it in the air, and laughed. "I'd hoped not to have to use my wand for anything other than wishes, but . . ."

Ruby reacted as if she'd been shocked with a bolt of powerful magic. "Gah!" she howled. "Don't turn me into a pumpkin, Ms. B! I'm sitting down." She flopped down next to Milla. "This stinks. I'm an ace at trivia. I could totally tromp Henry's friends. And my brother would owe me big-time for saving the family name."

Milla laughed. She loved being around Ruby and Henry—they seemed to have a lot of fun together. They were always joking and laughing and teasing each other. She got to have fun goofing around with Chip, but it definitely wasn't the same as having a twin brother.

"Want to learn to finger-knit instead?" Zahra offered, leaning over the back of the seat. "I brought a bunch of yarn. We could make something fun together."

"What *is* finger knitting?" Piper asked.

"Let me show you." Zahra gave each of them different-colored balls of yarn, and for much of the drive, they all worked on getting the hang of it. Zahra showed them how to weave the yarn around their fingers and then how to slide the loops up and over their fingertips to create a little stitch. Soon they all had a few inches of knotted yarn that Zahra suggested she could stitch together into a new hat for Piper.

When they were forty-five minutes away from camp, the bus stopped to let everyone stretch their legs and use the bathroom. As they loaded back into the bus, Milla realized Ruby was a lot quieter than usual. Ruby settled into the seat by the window and pulled her baseball cap down low on her forehead. "Are you okay?" Milla asked, sliding in beside her. Ruby nodded but said nothing.

It wasn't until the bus was moving that Milla realized something: Ruby's track pants had a white stripe running down the leg, but she was pretty sure Ruby had been wearing *plain* black pants when they'd boarded the bus. Milla looked more closely at Ruby's silhouette and began to laugh. "Henry?" she said quietly.

Henry peeked over and grinned mischievously. "Hi."

"Did you . . . ?" Milla broke off, giggling.

"Don't tell Roo I said this, but she really is the smarter twin," Henry whispered. "I wasn't about to let Levi beat me in trivia, so she and I swapped spots." He grinned. "She wants to win trivia, and I've always wanted to learn how to finger-knit."

Milla laughed even harder. "You really want to finger-knit?"

"My mom's birthday is coming up," Henry

said. "She appreciates homemade treasures."

"Okay," Milla said. She poked Zahra's shoulder and gestured to Henry. "Hey, Zahra? *Ruby* needs another lesson in finger knitting. She forgot how to do it."

Neither Zahra nor Piper realized that "Ruby" was very much *not* Ruby anymore. Milla waited for one of the other girls to figure out that the twins had switched places, but neither one did. In fact, no one noticed that it was Henry who unloaded Ruby's bag from the bus when they arrived at camp. Nor did anyone realize it was Henry who walked quietly alongside Milla and the others to the camp dining room. Milla couldn't believe the Fawcett twins had somehow managed to fool the whole fifth grade! They didn't look *that* much alike.

It was only when everyone sat down with their activity groups to eat lunch that Ms. Bancroft realized she had an imposter at her table. "Ruby," Ms. Bancroft said, trying to hide a laugh. "You've been very quiet since we got off the bus. Is anything the matter?"

Just then, the real Ruby strolled over from her brother's table in the camp dining room. "Busted," she said with a grin. She high-fived Henry and said, "But I totally rocked trivia for you, bro. You owe me."

Henry grinned. "Thanks, Roo." When he noticed Milla looking curiously at them, Henry shrugged. He bent down and said quietly, "You'd be surprised how often we get away with this. I have to keep my mouth shut when we swap spots, but Ruby's *really* good at imitating me. We manage to fool at least one person pretty much every time."

A few people started clapping about their prank, so Henry and Ruby stood in front of the class and took a deep bow. Milla clapped louder than anyone. They had only been at Adventure Camp for an hour, but things were already off to a very exciting start!

Ruby's Journal

Here's my question: Why princesses, Ms. B? Dresses make me itch, I don't like to dance, and I certainly don't want to get married to some guy with perfect hair and live in a big, cold castle.

You know what I do want to do? I want to be a famous athlete. When people talk about the greatest athletes of all time (Mia Hamm, Michael Jordan, Serena Williams, Brett Favre, Gabby Douglas, Michael Phelps) I want MY name to be on that list. Just put it right up at the top: RUBY FAWCETT.

But here's the problem: You know who doesn't want that? My dad. Sure, he's all about me practicing hard and doing my best, but since he's Mr. Know-It-All about college sports (in case you don't know this, Dad was sort of a big deal when he played college football), he always tells me it's more important to focus on my homework since a good education will serve me much better later in life.

Yeah, yeah, I'm getting way off the subject. Okay, so if I'm going to pick a Disney Princess I'm inspired by, I think I need to go with Mulan. I guess I've always thought of her as more warrior than princess, but . . . I guess she's actually both, right? Here's what I love about Mulan: she is super tough, and she sacrifices herself to save her family. It must have been really hard to go from tea-serving lessons to convincing everyone that she's a guy who can <u>fight.</u>

So I pick Mulan, Ms. B. That's my final answer. She shoots; she scores!

And you know what? I totally respect Mulan for how long she tricks people into thinking she's a guy. Henry and I have fun trading places sometimes, but someone usually figures it out pretty quickly. (To tell you the truth, I think Henry is the problem. He can never pretend to be me without cracking up. But I'm a total pro at acting like Hen. I just grunt a lot and talk really loud!)

11
COMPASS CHAMP

The cabins at Adventure Camp were huge, so the Daring Dreamers Club would be sharing a bunkhouse with girls from two other activity groups and their chaperones. All the log cabins were set about two hundred feet from each other, along a wooded path through the forest. Each cabin had twelve sets of bunk beds and a separate sleep loft for the adult chaperones and teachers.

Milla decided that the coolest thing about their cabins was that she would get to sleep in a top bunk! She had never slept in a bunk bed before, and she had certainly never slept in a bed frame that was made of giant logs. She spread out her sleeping bag, taped a picture of Chocolate Chip to the edge of her bunk (and gave it a quick kiss), and then climbed back down to tie her sneakers for the first Adventure Camp activity.

Ms. Bancroft led the group from their cabin along the path in the woods, back to the central campfire area. That was where they would be meeting with a counselor to start their first activity. The fifth grade had been split into three groups of about twenty-five kids each. These groups would take turns rotating from activity to activity throughout their time at camp.

While they walked through the woods to meet up with the others, Ms. Bancroft taught the Daring Dreamers Club a silly song about bullfrogs and then showed them how they could all come in at different times to turn the song into a round. Milla decided this was a fun extra perk that came with having the music teacher as their advisor.

"Welcome to Adventure Camp!" a counselor

said, once their group was gathered at the fire pit. Everyone cheered. "My name is Peter, and I'm going to be working with you guys today and tomorrow. We have a lot of fun planned for you while you're here. We'll be canoeing and visiting the high-ropes course later today, so I hope you're all excited about those two activities."

Milla glanced over at Mariana, who gave her a confident thumbs-up. Milla remembered Mari saying she was afraid of heights, but Mariana didn't seem to be letting her fear affect her at all. Milla admired Mariana's courage and willingness to try the ropes course, even though she was probably terrified.

"After a day full of activities, you'll enjoy a delicious dinner, as well as tasty s'mores, and skits by the campfire. But first!" Peter jabbed his finger into the air and hollered, "Let's start with outdoor adventure and survival skills!"

Everyone cheered again.

"Who knows what this little doohickey is?"

Peter held up a small plastic rectangle.

Milla put her hand in the air. "A compass," she said.

"Yes!" Peter said. "It is a compass." He asked everyone to break into groups of two, then gave each pair a compass. After he taught them all how to read the numbers, letters, and lines on the compass, Peter showed them how they could use it to find their way through the woods. "Have any of you ever heard of a sport called orienteering?"

Milla had. She looked around to see if anyone else would raise his or her hand. Piper, who was Milla's partner, nudged her and whispered, "I can tell you know what he's talking about. Say something!"

Milla put her hand in the air and said, "Orienteering is kind of like a scavenger hunt where you use a compass and a map for navigation." She had read about orienteering in a magazine article and had always thought it sounded fun.

"That's exactly right," Peter said, smiling at Milla. "Today we're going to do an orienteering activity to practice compass and map-reading skills. But that's not *all* you'll be doing. . . . You'll also be racing each other through the woods!" He gave each pair of fifth graders a laminated map of the Adventure Camp grounds, briefly explaining what all the symbols and lines meant. By studying the map, they could see where there were hills, lakes and streams, footpaths, and other important landmarks. Then Peter handed each group a smaller piece of paper with a bunch of funny-looking numbers on it.

"Every group now has an Adventure Camp map, along with a list of coordinates that will lead you to six different hot spots on our grounds. Each hot spot has a set of flags. If you follow the map and the directions correctly, you'll be able to collect a different-colored flag from each hot spot. Stop one is stocked with red flags, stop two has blue, stop three is green, and so on." Peter held up six colored flags to show the groups what they were searching for. "There are enough of each colored flag for every pair to take one at every stop."

"If you *don't* follow the directions or use your compass correctly," Peter explained, "you won't find the hot spots or the flags—but you will have a fun, scenic hike through the woods. The first team to reach the finish line with all six different-colored flags will be crowned today's Adventure Camp compass champions! The champions will get to be first in line at dinner tonight, and you will be given elegant, one-of-a-kind Adventure Camp crowns of honor to wear for the rest of the night."

Everyone laughed and began talking excitedly. Milla *really* wanted to be crowned Adventure Camp compass champion! She had read plenty of books about how to use a compass and was pretty sure she'd have no trouble with the activity. This was just the kind of thing she felt she was prepared for. She studied the instructions, trying to figure out which way she and Piper needed to go first. Their first set of directions said:

HOT SPOT #1
Bearing: 186°
Paces: 20

She glanced over at Mariana and Zahra's paper. The first set of coordinates on their paper was totally different. Milla guessed everyone's hot spots were listed in a different order so they didn't all just follow each other on their scavenger hunt through the woods.

"Something important to know," Peter said, "the word 'pace' means two *regular* steps. Not giant leaps or anything. Follow your compass and count your steps as you walk. Make sense?" Everyone nodded. Peter went on, "There are emergency whistles attached to each of the compasses. If anyone gets lost in the woods—and I mean *really* lost, not just a little turned around—blow three short blasts and one of the counselors will come find you. If you reach the fence that marks the outside of our camp property, don't go past it. If you stay inside the fence, you shouldn't have any trouble. Good luck. You may begin!"

Milla held the compass flat and turned until the compass was pointing at 186 degrees. She passed the paper and compass to Piper and said, "I think we need to go this way first. What do you think?" Milla looked at Piper to see if they were in agreement . . . and that was when she noticed that her partner looked a little anxious.

"What's wrong?" Milla whispered.

"I lost my glasses," Piper said.

Milla groaned. "You *lost* them?"

"I think I forgot them in the cabin. I was busy setting up my sleeping bag, and then we had to leave for the first activity, and I just, I don't know, set them down or something? I honestly didn't notice I wasn't wearing them until we were almost to the meeting spot, and I didn't want to turn around and make everyone late."

"Can you see *anything*?" Milla asked. "How did you not notice you weren't wearing them?

"My mind was on other stuff," Piper said. "I can see distances okay. But the map and compass are both just blurred colors and lines. I can't read the numbers at all."

Milla noticed that the other groups had already scattered. A few pairs of kids were charging through the woods, well on their way to their first hot spots. But some kids seemed to be having more trouble than others reading the numbers on their compasses. Henry and Ruby, who had teamed up, were pointing in opposite directions. Zahra and Mariana were working together, and Milla cringed when she noticed that Mari was holding the compass upside down.

"If you can't see anything, you're not going to learn anything about using a compass," Milla told Piper. She was happy to lead Piper through the woods, but it wouldn't be nearly as much fun if Piper could only see blurry outlines of stuff. "If Ms. Bancroft says it's okay, maybe we could run back to the cabin and grab your glasses? We'll get a late start on the activity, but at least you'll get to do it with everyone else."

"There's no way we'll win if we have to go back to the cabin before we start," Piper said. "And I really want to win."

"I do, too," Milla agreed, laughing. "But we'll have much more fun on the adventure if you can see where you're going. Come on! We're getting your glasses."

After getting the go-ahead from Ms. Bancroft,

Milla and Piper raced back to their cabin. They grabbed Piper's glasses, which were somehow all the way at the bottom of her sleeping bag, and then they ran back down the hill to start the compass challenge. All the other groups were way ahead of them, but Milla wasn't about to let a late start keep them from trying.

She and Piper made a great team. It only took them a few minutes to find their first hot spot and grab one of the red flags hanging from a low post in the middle of the woods. The next set of directions (Bearing: 65°—Paces: 35) took them up and over a hill with an amazing view of the high-ropes course. They grabbed a blue flag there and then raced through the woods to their third hot spot, which was near the lake where they would go canoeing later that day. The next set of flags was tucked inside a fence post right at the edge of the camp property. To get to the fifth hot spot, they had to pick their way through a dense part of the forest.

"Aren't you glad you have your glasses for this? You wouldn't have seen anything during our hike, and you'd be falling all over everything in the forest."

"Thanks, Milla," Piper said, draping her arm across Milla's shoulder. By the time they got to the sixth and final stop, there were only two flags left. They were obviously one of the last groups to find the hot spot. As Piper grabbed one of the yellow flags hanging from the post, she hugged Milla and said, "I'm sorry I kept us from winning."

"It's okay. We make a good team," Milla said, hugging her back. "Especially when you can see."

By the time they reached the finish line, all the other teams were already back. No one had gotten lost. Ruby and Henry had only found two hot spots and collected two flags, but they looked like they'd had a good time anyway.

"It's time to crown our Adventure Camp compass champions!" Peter said. "After a bit of a rocky start, these two compass masters proved they deserve this elegant reward." Peter held up two crowns made of recycled cardboard and tape. They were decorated with markers in a fun, colorful pattern. In a loud voice, he hollered, "Congratulations to Mariana and Zahra!" and then dropped the crowns atop their heads.

12
SURVIVAL SKILLS

As soon as they had finished the orienteering activity, the group gathered back at the fire pit and learned about other outdoor survival skills. First, Peter explained that it was very important to find fresh water if you were ever lost in nature. Then he taught the fifth graders how to build a small shelter out of fallen trees and branches. "If you're ever stuck outside," he said, "it's important to build some sort of shelter that can help protect you from the elements."

"Is a little stick fort really going to keep you warm in the middle of winter?" Henry asked.

"Anyone know why a shelter is a good idea *any* time of year?" Peter asked.

Milla raised her hand. Peter pointed to her, and she explained, "Even a simple shelter will help keep out the wind. On a hot day, it might shield you from the sun. And if it were to snow or rain, it would be nice to have a place you could try to stay a little drier."

Peter looked impressed. "It seems we have someone in this group who really knows her stuff. I couldn't have said it better myself. What's your name?"

"Milla." She felt her face flush. But in a good way, not in the way it sometimes flushed when people were obviously staring at her because of her scar. At times like that, she wanted to hide. Now, with her classmates and Ms. Bancroft and Peter looking at her in a very *different* way—as if she was someone who really knew her stuff—she was filled with pride. "Also, in cold weather you could try to build a small fire just outside the shelter, which would help you stay warm."

"Well, Milla," Peter said, laughing. "I feel like I should turn this class right over to you."

"She reads a lot of survival books," Piper blurted out. "I mean, a *lot*. Her nose is always in some adventure story or another."

"Well, all that reading has paid off," Peter said. He rubbed his hands together. "In fact, Milla's last comment leads me right into the next thing we need to talk about: building a fire."

Peter took a few minutes to talk about fire safety and showed them all how to clear a space that would safely contain a fire. He then gave each activity group leader a box of matches and asked them to work with their teams to figure out how to start a small fire. The challenge was that each group could only use *one* match, so they had to work together to get the fire set up just right before they tried to ignite it.

Ms. Bancroft insisted that her group do the work themselves, without any help from her. So the Daring Dreamers Club quickly appointed Milla their activity leader. Milla wasn't often the leader in groups, but she felt ready for the challenge.

"Okay," Milla said, getting right down to business. "First, we need to gather some bark or something else that will catch fire easily. We put that in the middle, along with some very small twigs and sticks to use as kindling. And then we should build a little tepee out of broken branches around the outside." As she spoke, she showed everyone examples of fire starters and kindling.

All five girls set off into the woods and gathered bark and kindling from the forest floor, along with some small broken sticks and branches to build a campfire tepee. A few minutes into the activity, Ruby started singing, *"Whistle while you work . . ."* The other four girls sang along, *"Come on, now, let us whistle while we whistle while we work!"*

Ms. Bancroft laughed. "Ah, I see my princess

assignment seems to have rubbed off on you!" She pulled her wand out of her backpack, pointed it at the group's small pile of sticks and branches, and whispered, "Bibbity-bobbity-boo!" Of course, nothing happened—but it made them all laugh.

When they decided everything was ready, Ms. Bancroft gave Milla the group's one and only match to try to light their fire. The whole Daring Dreamers Club cheered like crazy when their kindling ignited and the fire blazed to life.

After a quick snack of watermelon, Peter showed everyone how to put out the fires using

water. He told them they could also use snow, depending on the season. Then they walked over to the high-ropes course.

The course was in a giant clearing in the huge pine forest. Narrow wires and ropes stretched between trees and platforms, crisscrossing overhead. The course began with a long wooden ladder and ended in a forty-foot zip line that ran from the top of a tall platform down to the ground. Milla looped her arm through Mariana's. "You ready?"

"I think so." Mariana nodded, but Milla thought she looked a little pale. "Honestly?" Mari confessed a moment later. "I'm a little freaked out. Or maybe a *lot* freaked out. It looks super fun, but my heart is beating like crazy and we're still on solid ground!"

"You're going to do great," Milla promised. "I'll help distract you."

Both girls stepped into their harnesses and clipped on their helmets. Once they were hooked in, the instructors did a safety check. After a short lesson, the instructors let everyone go through the course at their own pace. Henry and Ruby were at the front of the pack, racing to be the first to finish. Zahra and Piper were toward the middle of the group. Mari and Milla watched as everyone clipped special locking metal loops called carabineers onto the safety wire and then climbed up a ladder to start the course.

"Go ahead," Mari told Milla. "I don't want to hold anyone up, so I think I should go last."

"Nope, I'm sticking with you," Milla told her. When Mari began to protest, Milla shook her head. "I *want* to. I've got your back."

Mari swallowed. She took a deep breath. "Okay. Here goes."

Mariana climbed up the ladder first. Milla followed, and she could see that Mari's legs were shaking. When her foot slipped near the top, she let out a tiny scream. But she caught her balance and made it up to the platform. As they side-stepped across the first narrow wire between two enormous trees, Milla distracted Mari by asking her questions about swim team.

Then they talked about Mariana's *abuela*—who she visited in Mexico every year—while stepping carefully across a series of wooden platforms.

Milla told Mari funny stories about Chip while the two girls scooted on all fours through a tunnel that swung high above the ground, suspended between two trees.

Before long, they had reached the final platform. "You're a pro," Milla assured her friend. "All that's left is to jump off and enjoy the ride back down to the ground." Milla helped Mari clip her carabineer onto the zip line and then gave her a reassuring smile.

"Jump," Mari said boldly. "All right!" When Milla looked over, she saw that Mariana was squeezing her lips together, and her body was frozen at the edge of the platform. She was staring straight down, her face a mask of terror. "Okay!"

Mari's voice was squeaking. "Here goes. Right *now*." Still, she didn't move.

"Think of it this way," Milla said. "It's just like bouncing off the diving board or the starting blocks at the pool." She looked down to the ground and saw Ms. Bancroft and the other three members of the Daring Dreamers Club waiting for them at the end. Milla waved, and they all cheered. "Except instead of water, you're jumping into a pool of friends!"

Mariana laughed, her face relaxing just slightly. "You're right. Okay. I made it this far," she said. "There's no reason I can't finish. Look out below!" Then Mari took a deep breath, grabbed the clasp above her head, and jumped.

Mariana

When you come from a family of swimmers, your blood is at least half chlorine. There's no place I feel more at home than on the pool deck or in the pool. So I guess it's pretty obvious that Ariel is the princess I connect with most. But it's not just because she swims and lives in the water. Like Ariel, I often feel like a fish out of water when I'm on dry land. I would love to join theater this year, but I guess I'm a little scared I might flop around like a total klutz onstage, because sometimes it feels like I have fins instead of feet.

My mom is always reminding me that long legs and arms are really helpful for swimming, but it's sometimes hard being the tallest kid in the fifth-grade class. It seems like my body doesn't always work the way I want it to, and I stand out all the time! I also feel really shy when I'm away from the pool (the sea witch didn't steal my voice, like she did with Ariel, but sometimes it feels that way).

I know everyone else was really excited about Adventure Camp, but I've been sort of nervous about this trip. I don't have a lot of friends at school. My closest buds are from the swim team and go to other schools, and I was a little worried about not having anyone to hang out with. But now that we have the Daring Dreamers Club, it feels like I have a team at school. I love having a group of friends this year. We're all really different, but that's what makes it fun to be together.

It's easier to try new things when you know someone has your back!

:)

13
PADDLE, PADDLE, PLOP

The lake at Adventure Camp was shallow, marshy, and surrounded by tall grasses. The shoreline snaked and bent, making the narrow lake look more like a twisting river. Milla had studied the map during their orienteering exercise and knew the lake was shaped a little like the letter "L"—long and skinny, with a bend at one end. The boat launch was right at the very top of the L.

When the group was gathered at the shore, Peter asked everyone to find a life jacket that fit them. Then he explained how to hold a paddle and talked a bit about water safety. "Each of your life jackets is equipped with a whistle, just like the compasses," Peter told them. "It would be nearly impossible for anyone to get lost on this lake. It's just not that big. But everyone has a whistle, just in case."

"In case of what?" Ruby asked.

Peter chuckled. "We have had a few groups fall into the water over the years, but that's very unusual. I don't expect any of you to go overboard. The canoes are stable. Just remember to sit still, stay in the center of the boat, and paddle calmly."

Piper leaned toward Milla and whispered, "If anyone falls into this lake, it's going to be me. Am I right?"

Milla laughed and whispered back, "You're not going to fall in."

"Five bucks?" Piper said.

"You want to *bet* on whether you're going to fall in?" Milla asked. "It's a deal. Five bucks says you're not going to fall in. I have faith in you."

Piper blinked and looked surprised. "Thanks, Milla. That's a really nice thing to say."

Peter talked for a while about the dos and don'ts of canoeing; then he told everyone to break into groups of two or three. Each group would paddle together to the far end of the lake, then turn their canoe around and paddle back. "For some of you, this task won't take long at all, and you'll have some time to relax out on the water. For others, it will be more of a challenge." Peter clipped on his own life jacket and slid the first canoe into the water. "Just do your best. It's not a race; this activity is about practicing skills and having fun. Enjoy yourselves out there. Remember to look around and take in a different view of the woods from the water."

There were dozens of silver canoes lined up along the shore. One by one, Peter helped the groups load into their canoes and then pushed them out into the lake. "If there are three of you in a group, take turns paddling. The extra person can sit in the middle for now. There's a dock at the other end of the lake—you should hop out and swap seats when you get there so everyone can give paddling a try. I'll stay toward the middle of the group to keep an eye on how things are going."

Piper and Mariana went together in one canoe, so Milla, Ruby, and Zahra teamed up in another. "I don't mind sitting in the middle first," Milla told them. "I can navigate!"

"Are you sure?" Zahra asked. "I don't know what I'm doing."

"Me either," Ruby seconded.

"None of us are experts," Milla said, settling in on a slim seat in the middle of the canoe. "We'll figure it out."

It took a little while for Zahra to get the hang of the paddle, but it wasn't long before she was moving it through the water like a pro. And Ruby, who seemed to be good at every sport, was a natural. In just a few minutes, the three girls had put quite a bit of distance between their canoe and the rest of the group. Henry and Levi were close for a while, but the guys lost some ground when they both started paddling on the same side, making their canoe spin in circles.

Ruby called to her brother over her shoulder. "Hey, Henry, race you to the far end of the lake!" Without waiting for a response, she began paddling like mad.

The canoe rocked from side to side, and Milla had to hold on to the boat to steady herself. "Ruby, slow down," Milla laughed. "It's not supposed to be a race, remember?"

"But it would be kind of nice to get to the other end of the lake first, right?" Ruby asked. "Zahra's the only one of us who's won an activity today. Hey, Zahra!"

Zahra spun around. "Yeah?"

"Let's see how fast we can get this thing to go," Ruby suggested. "Then we'll have some time to kick our feet up and rest when we get to the far end of the lake. You said you wanted to relax in nature, right?"

"Okay," Zahra said, shrugging. Milla had noticed that Zahra was almost always willing to go with the flow—it was one of her favorite things about her new friend.

It didn't take long for Zahra and Ruby to get a really good rhythm going. Soon their canoe was zooming through the lake. The sounds of their classmates' voices faded; after a few minutes, even Levi and Henry were far behind. By the time they reached the L bend in the lake and steered their canoe around the corner, Milla looked back and realized they had lost sight of everyone else. Ruby and Zahra paddled a little farther, stopping about a hundred feet from the dock at the far end of the lake.

"Ahhh," Ruby said. "Time to relax!" She dropped her paddle, picked up a pair of binoculars, and slid to the left side of the canoe. The long silver canoe rocked as Ruby's weight shifted. For a moment Milla worried it might tip.

Milla tried to keep her weight centered as they bobbed along in the calm water. The only sounds were birdcalls from high up in the trees and the shushing sound of the wind in the grasses at the edge of the lake.

"This is perfect," Zahra said. "Mariana was right—canoeing is lovely. Everything looks so different from out here on the water."

Milla scanned the shoreline, hoping they might spot a deer or some other wildlife. But it was hard to see past the tall grasses into the woods. So Milla leaned carefully over one side of the boat. She peered into the water. Was that something moving below them? She tried to get her eyes to adjust to the dark, murky water. "Hey, guys, is that . . . ," she began. Yes, there it was again. Something was definitely moving through the water under their boat. "A turtle!"

Milla leaned farther over the edge of the

canoe. A painted turtle was paddling through the water, just a few feet under their boat.

Everything happened quickly after that. Milla leaned. Ruby leaned. Zahra stood up to get a better look into the water. The canoe tilted and shifted as they all peered over the same side of the boat. Milla tried to rebalance their weight by leaning the *other* way. But instead, the sudden shift made the canoe rock first to one side, then the other.

As the canoe wobbled, Zahra lost her footing. She windmilled her arms in the air, trying to stop herself from falling. But it was too late—the canoe was already rolling. Before anyone had time to realize what was happening, all three girls plopped into the water.

14
TURTLE TROUBLE

Milla and Zahra bobbed side by side in the lake. "Are you okay?" Milla asked her friend.

"I'm fine," Zahra said. She started laughing uncontrollably. "I said I wanted some time to relax out here in the lake . . . but I didn't mean literally *in* the lake." Milla cracked up, too, but she stopped laughing when she heard Ruby scream.

"Help!" About ten feet away from the other two girls, Ruby was flailing her arms in the water. "Someone help!"

Milla kicked over to her. "Are you hurt?" She searched the top of her life jacket for the whistle she was supposed to blow in an emergency.

"No, I'm not hurt," Ruby screamed. "But there's a *turtle* somewhere in the water near me!"

"Other than the turtle, you're okay?" Milla said, clasping the whistle between her fingers and holding it close to her lips. Ruby nodded. "The turtle is harmless," Milla told her. "Small painted turtles are very gentle creatures, and they aren't much bigger than a human hand." There was absolutely nothing to be scared of in the lake—but clearly, Ruby thought otherwise.

"It's going to eat me!" Ruby screamed. "I can feel it touching my leg. Help! Get it off! Get it away from me!"

Milla realized Ruby was in full-on panic mode. And she knew that panicking was *not* the best way for them to get out of their current situation. "Ruby," she said as soothingly as she could, "you have to stay calm. Take a deep breath and let your life jacket do its job."

Ruby took a shallow breath and stared at

Milla with an anxious expression on her face. She sucked in another tiny gasp of air.

"Good," Milla said. "Can you take another, *deeper* breath?"

Ruby took another small breath, then another slightly deeper one. Just as she began to breathe normally, her cotton headband slipped down over her eyes. When she reached up to push it out of the way, she splashed water all over her own face and began to freak out again.

Zahra swam over to them. Her headscarf was soaked with lake water, and Milla thought it

probably felt cold and very heavy. But Zahra had a huge smile on her face, so Milla knew she was okay.

"Listen," Milla said gently, more for Ruby's benefit than Zahra's. "We're going to be just fine. This is why we're wearing life jackets. We could float here for hours if we needed to."

"*Hours?*" Ruby screeched.

"But we *won't* be here for hours," Milla promised. One of her favorite adventure stories was a series of books about a group of rangers who worked in the Boundary Waters Canoe Area Wilderness. She had learned more than she would ever need to know about canoeing and boat safety from reading those books. "The cool thing about canoes is that they float even when they're filled with water. Look."

Milla put her hand on the edge of the aluminum canoe. Although the boat was almost completely filled with water, it was still floating just above the surface.

"So what are we supposed to do?" Zahra asked.

"It will be a little awkward," Milla began, "but we can actually sit inside the sunken canoe. It will separate you from the turtle, Ruby."

"Then what?" Ruby whimpered.

"We'll paddle over to the dock, just over there, and wait for some help emptying out our boat," Milla said. She blew her whistle, but then she decided it was silly to just sit there waiting for help when they could save themselves in the meantime. Still, she really hoped she was doing the right thing.

Milla and Zahra collected the two paddles, which had started to float away from the submerged canoe. Then she and Ruby held on to one side of the boat while Zahra held on to the other. On the count of three, the girls climbed back into the wobbling, water-filled canoe. Though they were sitting chest-deep in water, the canoe was floating. Milla suggested that Ruby sit in the middle of the canoe while she and Zahra paddled them toward the dock.

By the time Peter and the rest of the group arrived a few minutes later, the girls were scrambling out of the canoe and onto the dock. All three of them were soaked but smiling.

"Why'd you decide to take a swim in your clothes, Roo?" Henry yelled. "I think falling in disqualifies you from the race!"

Ruby shivered and glared at her brother.

"Ahhh, this dry shirt sure does feel good," Henry taunted. He grinned at Ruby and asked, "Who's the smart twin now?"

Milla hugged her knees to her chest and grinned. She had wanted adventure—and she'd certainly gotten it. Milla thought back to what her moms had told her: that very few adventures go as planned. That had *definitely* been proven true today!

15
ADVENTURE AWAITS

After dinner that night, as the rest of the fifth graders set off toward the campfire pit for skits and s'mores, Ms. Bancroft asked her group to hang back in the dining room. "We'll join the others soon," she began. "I just wanted to take a moment to tell you all how proud I am of you."

"Thanks, Ms. B!" Ruby said. "But, um, for what, exactly? Falling in the lake?"

Ms. Bancroft chuckled. "All of you have faced challenges today," she said. "Some of those challenges were a bit, well, *wetter* than others. But you have handled every obstacle set before you with grace and smarts. But most importantly, you've proven time and again that you know how to work as a team. I just wanted to say that I'm proud to be your advisor, and I'm excited about the adventures we have ahead of us this year."

Zahra leaned over and gave Ms. Bancroft a hug. Milla did the same.

Ms. B continued, "I know some of you were a little resistant to my princess journal assignment, but I really appreciate that you've all put some thought into your entries. I feel like I'm getting to know you, and I hope you all feel like you're getting to know each other better."

"Actually, Ms. B?" Ruby blurted. "I had fun picking my princess. Yeah, I was a little down on the assignment at first, but after I figured out what you were asking us to do, it was fun. It kind of feels like I have a secret identity: Mulan Fawcett!" She grinned. "Thinking about Mulan is what gave me the idea to swap places with Henry on the bus. A brilliant idea, if I do say so myself."

"I liked the princess assignment, too," Mariana agreed. "I keep thinking about how much I feel like Ariel, trying to find my way in a new world with all of you. New year, new friends, new experiences. I don't usually like writing about myself, but it's been easier, somehow, because I'm writing about Ariel."

"I thought it was an interesting assignment," Zahra said. "I liked the way your question made me think about myself."

"Same here," Milla said. "And there have even been a few times this week when I've thought about how Belle would act in a certain situation."

Ms. Bancroft looked thrilled that her assignment had turned out to be so popular. Milla was happy to hear that the other girls had enjoyed the writing assignment as much as she had. Ms. Bancroft glanced at Milla and said, "Milla, you wrote something interesting in your last journal entry that I'd love to share with the rest of the group. Would that be okay with you?"

Milla nodded.

"Milla wrote in her journal," Ms. Bancroft began, "that it can sometimes be hard to see the best parts of yourself, unless someone else points them out to you. I happen to agree. One of the things that I wish for this year is that you'll all use your journal writing and your friends in this group to discover new talents, uncover hidden strengths, and support one another as you set out to achieve your dreams."

"Hear, hear!" Piper hollered. She took a deep breath. "And speaking of dreams . . . I was going to tell you about this at our next Daring Dreamers meeting, but I guess there's no point in waiting." She drummed her hands on the dining room table and said, "So yesterday when I got home from school, my dad told me about auditions for a kids' cooking show. Anyone want to help me get the part?"

They all whooped and shouted "Yes!"

One of the camp cooks poked his head out

of the kitchen and asked, "Everything okay out here?"

Piper waved at him. "All good! Just dreaming big. Nothing dangerous. Carry on!" The cook shook his head and stepped back into the kitchen.

With a laugh, Ms. B stood up, gestured to the door outside, and said, "Shall we join the others?"

"Let's get out there!" Milla cheered. Then the six of them linked arms and stepped out into the great wide somewhere . . . ready to continue their adventures together.

Milla

Once upon a time, there was a girl who dreamed of a life filled with adventure . . . and after years of dreaming, her wishes have finally started to come true!

Even if Adventure Camp didn't go exactly the way I was expecting it to, I had a <u>great</u> time. The best thing is, now I know for sure that I can take care of myself in just about any situation! Of course, there were more than a few bumps along the way. But like my moms said, it wouldn't be much of an adventure if everything went according to plan.

I'm not the kind of girl who's ever been a big fan of stories that end with a boring old "happily ever after." You know why? Because those words mean the story is ending right when you get to the good stuff! Sure, this adventure is soon going to come to an end. But I'm pretty sure Adventure Camp is the first of many adventures to come.

I've only just started my story. I can't wait to write (and live!) the rest of it.

Author's Note

When I was a kid, I was obsessed with *The Little Mermaid*. I loved Ariel's sense of adventure, and like her, I longed to explore and learn about unfamiliar new worlds. For several years, I dreamed of one day going to space camp, with the hope that someday I would become an astronaut.

My idol throughout much of elementary school was Sally Ride, the first American woman to travel into space. Ms. Ride applied to be an astronaut, while she was still in college. She was chosen to join the space program in 1978, the first year women were invited to apply. Thanks to Ms. Ride, girls like me could imagine going to space someday . . . because she helped pave the way for future generations of women. After Ms. Ride retired from the astronaut program, she went on to be a professor and spent her life encouraging students—especially girls—to study math, science, and engineering.

As I got older, my dreams shifted. For a while, I wanted to be a marine biologist, then an Olympic swimmer, and for a few years I dreamed of becoming a famous actor. I'm lucky to be blessed with a very supportive family who have always encouraged me to dream big. My parents told me I could do anything I wanted to do if I worked hard and believed in myself. Because of their support, I never doubted that. I also had strong, smart female role models, like Sally Ride, my own mom (who was the first female wilderness ranger in the Forest Service!), and teachers and mentors like Ms. Bancroft in this book, who helped show me anything was possible.

The day I started working on this series, I went to an event where I heard polar explorer Ann Bancroft speak about her first dogsledding trip to the North Pole. As the only female member of the Steger International Polar Expedition in 1986, she became the first known woman in history to cross the ice to the North Pole. She took a leave of absence from her job as a public school teacher to pursue a lifelong dream of big adventures in the great wide somewhere. (Ann Bancroft's love of exploration inspired the character of Milla in this series!) In the years since that first trip to the Pole, Ann Bancroft has led many polar expeditions, including the first east-to-west crossing of Greenland by American women and the American Women's Expedition to the South Pole on *skis*!

In 1991, the real-life Ms. Bancroft started a foundation that provides financial support, inspiration, and resources to help young women reach, explore, and discover their own dreams. Ann Bancroft is dedicated to encouraging women and girls to pursue their dreams and help make them come true. Her lifelong commitment is the reason I named such an important character in this book after her—Ms. Bancroft's courage, teamwork, and leadership skills make her a wonderful role model for all women and girls.

. . .

Along with Ann Bancroft, there are many people who helped get this series off the ground. I'd like to take a moment to thank a few who were instrumental to the process.

First, thanks *very much* to Disney and Random House for allowing me to develop this group of girls and write such a fun series. I'm having a wonderful time exploring the inspiring world of Disney Princesses. Special thanks to the people working so hard on this series, notably my editors Rachel Poloski and Michelle Nagler at Random House, along with Lauren Burniac and Samantha McFerrin at Disney. Thanks also to the brand, marketing, sales, and design teams at both companies for all of your support and ideas.

High-fives to Norah Bestler, Mackenzie Bestler, and Genevieve Ganje for taking the time to tell me about your favorite Disney Princesses . . . and going into detail about exactly what makes them special. You shed a whole new light on Merida ("She's so strong and brave!"), Mulan ("She's super tough and smart—and rocks!"), and Belle ("She's always kind to people, which is the right way to be").

A smart group of readers—Norah Bestler, Stella Wedren, Ruby Downing, Milla Downing, Henry Downing, Frankie McConville, Barb Soderberg, and Samantha Thiegs (along with her mom, Lisa!)—commented on various versions of this first story and helped me develop all the characters in the series. Thanks, guys!

Jenn Sanders was my dinner companion one night at a National Convention of Teachers of English dinner, and over dessert, she wisely suggested that each book in this series include a short biography of one real woman who helped inspire a character. I took your excellent advice—thanks, Jenn!

Katra Ismail, the Somali Associate Educator at Washburn High School in Minneapolis, connected me with a wonderful group of young women who helped me to better understand important details of Somali culture and Islamic faith that allowed me to further develop Zahra's character. Thank you to Shehnaz Abdinzak, Aisha Ali, Shadia Nooh, Hafsa Hassan, and Ilhan Mire for taking time out of your busy school days to chat with me! Thanks also to Washburn Principal Rhonda Dean for welcoming me into your school. I'm also extremely grateful to David Lin and Bill Imada at IW Group, Inc., who carefully read and commented on this manuscript and provided thoughtful feedback on cultural issues. Finally, huge thanks to my friend Waqar Ahmad, who spent considerable time helping me to better understand Islamic faith and practices.

I got to do a *lot* of research on pet pigs (and pig rescue) while writing about Chocolate Chip. I went into this book thinking a pet pig would be cute and fun . . . and probably not much harder than having a dog around. I quickly realized just how wrong I was. Though they're cute, charming, and smart, pigs are also a *big* commitment, and people who take pigs in as pets often realize they've gotten in way over their heads. The most helpful source I found was teacuppig.info. I also enjoyed looking at lots of pig pictures and videos on Instagram every day!

Adventure Camp was inspired by my kids' third- and fourth-grade overnight field trips to Voyageur Environmental Center in Mound, Minnesota, and Deep Portage Conservation Reserve and Learning Center in Hackensack, Minnesota. Both centers are remarkable, and do a great job getting kids excited about outdoor activities!

As always, thanks to my agent—Michael Bourret—for all you do to help me achieve my big dreams as a writer.

Lastly, thanks to my family and friends—for holding my hand and helping me brainstorm, offering lots of cuddles, and cheering me on. I love you!

DON'T MISS THE NEXT BOOK IN THE SERIES!

PiPER COOKS UP A PLAN

TURN THE PAGE FOR A SNEAK PEEK . . .

1
COOKING UP CHAOS

Piper Andelman's experiment was going exactly as planned . . . until the smoke alarm went off.

Beeeeeep!

Beeeeeeep!

Beeeeeeep!

Piper pressed oven mitts over her ears, trying to block out the awful sound. "Nothing to worry about!" she hollered, even though her family probably couldn't hear her over the loud beeping. "Just a little smoke, but I'll have it cleared out in a sec!"

Moving quickly, Piper slid a charred, smoking

beaker away from the heat. She was turning off her hot plate when her dad, Jeremy, raced into the kitchen. He glanced around, grabbed a rolled-up newspaper off the counter, and fanned it under the wailing smoke detector. Piper flung open a window and waited for the smoke to clear.

In the midst of all the excitement, Piper's little sister, Finley, bounced around the kitchen, trying to capture everything on video with their dad's phone.

Piper's dad dropped the newspaper as soon as the smoke alarm stopped screaming. The silence was a welcome relief. "Things going well in here?" he asked in an even voice.

"All good," Piper said. She stood in front of her makeshift lab, holding her arms out wide to try to hide the chaos on the counter. Science was messy, but sometimes it was hard for parents to understand that. Especially when science took over the kitchen right before dinnertime.

Piper's dad peered around her, raising his eyebrows when he spotted the scorched beaker and a countertop covered in sticky, blue blobs. Nestled among the blobs was a mixing bowl filled with rising bread dough. A roasting pan full of chopped carrots, potatoes, and fresh herbs was ready to go into the oven.

"It's all good. Really," Piper repeated with a smile. She sighed and added, "Dinner will be ready as soon as Mom gets home from work. I just got bored while I was waiting for the bread dough to rise, so I decided to play around a little bit. I'm testing how temperature and cooking time impact the texture of hard candy."

"Uh-huh," her dad said, folding his arms over his chest. "And what did you discover?"

Piper glanced at the still-smoldering beaker and shrugged. "I have my hypothesis and have started conducting tests to see if I'm right. But I can't share the results, since I haven't finished my experiment. A true scientist doesn't trust a hunch, Dad. You know I've gotta prove it first."

Finley climbed onto the counter, balancing on all fours like a cat. She plucked one of the blue blobs off the counter and popped it into her mouth. The feisty six-year-old smacked her lips together as she sucked on the slightly chewy candy.

"Meow is helping," Finley told their dad. "Meow is the taste tester and the camera lady! Meow!" Finley was going through an animal phase. For the past week, she had been starting and finishing most of her sentences with a loud *meow*. Piper had decided this was an improvement over her sheep phase, when she would only say *"Baaaa."*

"I see," their dad said, a smile pulling at the corners of his mouth. With a nod at the counter, he said, "Thanks for cooking tonight." He raked a hand through his brown mop of curls. His checkered shirt was misbuttoned, and his glasses were smudged with fingerprints.

Piper glanced at her own messy outfit through

equally smudged glasses. There were sugary stains all over her apron, and she could feel her floppy knit panda hat sliding off one side of her head. It was no wonder people said she took after her dad.

"Have you both finished your homework?" Dad asked.

Piper took a deep breath but didn't answer. In Finley's kindergarten world, homework was a daily coloring sheet or alphabet worksheet. Fun and games, mostly. In fifth grade, homework was the pits.

When Piper wasn't using math for science experiments or measuring recipes, she found it a total chore—and a bore. Worksheets took all the *fun* out of math, and the word problems they had been working on for the past month were all so ridiculous. The questions never related to real-world problems, and the answers never made sense if you really thought about them. Piper had tried to point this out, but her teacher, Mr.

Mohan, didn't seem to want to hear it. The worst part was, it was extra hard for Piper to follow the math when there was so much reading involved.

Reading and writing had *always* been a challenge for Piper, because of her dyslexia. Math had continually seemed to take her a little longer than most people, as a result of how her mind worked. Even still, she'd never had too much trouble keeping up in math class before. But because of all the word problems they had been doing lately, Piper had started to seriously fall behind in math. And it seemed that the farther behind she fell, the harder her assignments and quizzes had gotten. Since her homework was never easy *or* fun, she could come up with a million other things she would rather be doing.

"I'll do my homework after dinner," Piper promised. "You know I need a brain break after school."

"Okay," her dad said, nodding. "I'll be in my office if you need me. This deadline is killing me."

He strolled out of the kitchen, trusting that Piper would clean up after herself. She always did. Well, *usually*. Or maybe it was more like *sometimes*. But she'd noticed her dad seemed extra stressed out about work recently, so she would definitely clean up today. She wanted to stay on his good side.

Piper's dad worked from home as a graphic designer, so his "office" was just a desk in the corner of the living room. Whenever he was working on a big project, Piper offered to make the family dinner. She loved to cook, so this was one of her favorite ways to help out. Piper wasn't the smartest or most athletic Andelman (that title went to her older brother, Dan); nor was she the cutest or funniest (Finley), so Piper worked hard to try to impress her parents in other ways.

Even though making family dinners was never as exciting as any of her other food-science experiments, Piper knew that every chance she got to fool around in the kitchen was an opportunity to learn something new. She considered herself part scientist, part chef. To Piper, the words "kitchen" and "lab" meant the same thing. After all, cooking was its own kind of science.

When Piper was baking or boiling something, she knew it was important to use the right ingredients, the correct amounts, the right temperatures, and the proper amount of time—just like any other kind of science experiment. If she got the mix wrong, dinner would be a bust . . . or blow up. (Dinner had only blown up once, and it was a very messy lesson learned!)

As soon as their dad had returned to the living room, Piper grabbed the phone out of her sister's sticky hands. "Let's see what you got," she said, hitting play on the video. Both girls giggled as they watched the footage of Piper's candy experiment. The smoke alarm was a nice touch. It gave the video some extra character.

Piper wasn't at all bothered by the fact that her experiment had gone up in smoke. In fact, she was pleased. Mistakes—in both science *and* cooking—taught you something, and oftentimes led to unexpected discoveries. Food science was all about testing things out and adjusting to find the right mix for your experiment. You could get different results every time and it was no big deal . . . unlike math, where making mistakes just led to a wrong answer.

"Do you think you have enough for your audition video meow?" Finley asked, popping a slice of carrot into her mouth. She made a face as she pulled a sprig of rosemary out of her mouth. "Icky prickly herbs," she said, spitting the carrot into the sink.

"Yeah," Piper said, nodding. "I should have more than enough. Thanks for helping, Fin." She washed her hands and pushed the rest of her equipment to the side while she finished preparing dinner. As she formed balls of dough into dinner rolls, she thought about how she would put her audition video together.

For the past few weeks, Piper had been working on an audition video for her favorite television
cooking competition, *The Future of Food*. The
TV show was touring around the country,
searching for the most innovative kid cooks in
America. Piper was thrilled when she found out
they would be filming an upcoming episode in a
nearby town. She had always wanted a chance to
try out for the show!

The Future of Food was different from most
cooking shows, because kids were expected to use
creativity and innovation in the kitchen, instead
of just cooking big, fancy meals in a traditional
way. Each week, the show had a different theme.
Sometimes, contestants were asked to cook or
bake using unusual cutting-edge gadgets. Other
times, the host of the show introduced a crazy,
out-there theme. Once, *The Future of Food* contestants had to cook without using any electronic
tools at all. Another time, contestants were told
that they lived in a future that only had potatoes

and cows—so they could *only* use potato and beef products in their dishes. One of Piper's favorite episodes had required contestants to cook in a space suit, using only freeze-dried astronaut food.

Each week, three lucky and talented kid cooks were invited to compete in *The Future of Food*'s kitchen. The winner of each week's show earned a $10,000 cash prize!

Being on a show like *The Future of Food* was one of Piper's big dreams, and she had every intention of making it come true. But even more importantly, she was going to win. Then she could finally prove to her family that *she* was the best at something, too!

2
DARING DREAMERS

"They picked me!" Piper blurted out, unable to keep her secret a moment longer. She had been waiting all day to share her huge news with the other four members of the Daring Dreamers Club. Now that their Tuesday advisory group meeting was officially in session, Piper bounced around Ms. Bancroft's classroom waving a piece of paper in the air. "I'm in! I'm going to be on *The Future of Food*!"

She held the sheet of paper in front of her nose and announced, "I got an email this morning that says, 'Congratulations, Piper Andelman!'

That's me! 'Based on the quality and creativity of your audition video, we would like to invite you to participate in an upcoming episode of *The Future of Food*.'" Piper twisted one of her braids and looked around. "Then it goes on and on with a whole bunch of details about dates and times, where I go for filming, and stuff like that. Can you believe it?"

"This is so exciting!" Milla Bannister-Cook said, squeezing her best friend tight. Sweet, adventure-loving Milla had been friends with Piper for years, so she knew just how much an opportunity like this meant to her. "When do they film the episode?"

"In less than three weeks," Piper told her friends. "I have a zillion things to do to get ready. I'm going to be cooking so much the next few weeks!"

"We'll help you!" Ruby Fawcett said, speaking on behalf of everyone. Ruby was the smallest member of the Daring Dreamers Club, but she had the biggest voice. In fact, Ruby and her twin brother, Henry, were two of the most outspoken—and sporty—members of the fifth-grade class at Walter Roy Elementary. Loyal, clever, tell-it-like-it-is Ruby was the kind of person everyone wanted on their team. "What can we do to make sure you're ready to win?"

"I can be a taste tester or a sous-chef, if you want," Mariana Sanchez offered with a shy smile. Though Mari was quiet, she was also one of the most fearless people Piper had ever met. She loved trying new things, and she was good at almost everything she tried. "I'm not a picky eater, and I'm pretty good at chopping. My *abuela* loves to cook, and she's taught me stuff. She makes the most amazing chicken mole you've ever eaten."

"You know Chip will happily eat any yucky scraps that aren't fit for human consumption," Milla said, laughing. Chocolate Chip was Milla's pet pig, and he loved snacking on Piper's creations—even the yucky, failed experiments. "I probably won't be much help with tasting, but I'd be happy to help with cleanup duties." Milla was allergic to nuts and dairy, so she had to be careful about what she ate.

"Can I help you figure out your outfit for the show?" Zahra Sharif asked. Hardworking, independent Zahra loved designing clothes, as well as making mosaics and painting in her free time. She was the most artistic member of the Daring Dreamers Club. "We have to find something for you to wear that's going to really pop on TV. And I would *love* to help you come up with some fun ideas for plating your food. Your dishes need to look creative and appealing if you want to win, right?"

The offers of help were shouted out, voices layering on top of voices, as everyone grew more and more excited about Piper's television debut. The Daring Dreamers Club had only been around since the first week of fifth grade, when the five girls were assigned to the same advisory group at school. But in that short time, Piper, Milla, Ruby, Zahra, and Mariana had already grown very close.

Advisory groups were something their school's principal had started to help fifth graders prepare for the independence of middle school. Every fifth grader was put in a small group made up of peers and a teacher-advisor. During their twice-weekly meetings, these groups talked about issues and challenges, goals and dreams.

Piper's group had been lucky enough to get Ms. Bancroft, the school's new music teacher, as their advisor. Ms. B was one of the most unique and inspiring women any of them had ever met. Ms. Bancroft loved encouraging her group to dream big and reach for the stars, and other stuff like that—which is why the girls had named themselves the Daring Dreamers Club.

Piper couldn't quite believe one of her big dreams was already coming true—and to make the dream even sweeter, she was going to *win*!

"Guess what?" she said, smiling wider. "I get enough guest passes that all of you will be able to come watch the show being filmed!" Everyone cheered.

Ms. Bancroft spoke for the first time that meeting. "I think I must be a little out of the loop . . . ," she said reluctantly. "What exactly is *The Future of Food*? Some sort of television show, I'm guessing?"

Ruby's mouth gaped open. "You haven't seen it, Ms. B?"

Ms. Bancroft shrugged. "I'm more of a movie buff. And frankly, cooking isn't my strong suit. I'm a canned soup and takeout kind of chef."

Piper groaned. "Whoa, whoa, whoa . . . You can't *cook*?"

"I didn't say I *can't*," Ms. Bancroft said, laughing. "I just prefer not to. My kitchen experiments never end well."

"Okay, this could be a problem," Piper said. One of the things that made *The Future of Food* fun was the host—who called herself the Kitchen Wizard—loved surprise challenges. Contestants never got to just *cook*. There was always some sort of twist.

Piper had watched every episode of *The Future of Food* and knew that the Kitchen Wizard sometimes even made contestants work with a friend or family member to create their dish. Piper wanted to be prepared for *anything* the show's host might throw at her, so she had to make sure her audience members were ready for the competition, too! What if they were called up to cook with her?

TO BE CONTINUED . . .